HEAVEN CAN WAIT

HEAVEN CAN WAIT

TIKI DURAND

TATE PUBLISHING
AND ENTERPRISES, LLC

Heaven Can Wait
Copyright © 2013 by Tiki Durand. All rights reserved.

No part of this publication may be reproduced, stored in a retrieval system or transmitted in any way by any means, electronic, mechanical, photocopy, recording or otherwise without the prior permission of the author except as provided by USA copyright law.

This novel is a work of fiction. Names, descriptions, entities, and incidents included in the story are products of the author's imagination. Any resemblance to actual persons, events, and entities is entirely coincidental.

The opinions expressed by the author are not necessarily those of Tate Publishing, LLC.

Published by Tate Publishing & Enterprises, LLC
127 E. Trade Center Terrace | Mustang, Oklahoma 73064 USA
1.888.361.9473 | www.tatepublishing.com

Tate Publishing is committed to excellence in the publishing industry. The company reflects the philosophy established by the founders, based on Psalm 68:11,
"The Lord gave the word and great was the company of those who published it."

Book design copyright © 2013 by Tate Publishing, LLC. All rights reserved.
Cover design by Allen Jomoc
Interior design by Ronnel Luspoc

Published in the United States of America

ISBN: 978-1-62295-336-3
1. Fiction / Christian / General
2. Fiction / Christian / Romance
12.10.09

Acknowledgments

Every good and perfect gift comes from you, Lord; it says so in your Word, James 1:17, and the ability to create through the use of words, I consider to be just that: a gift. So I thank you Lord for entrusting me with such a special assignment, to minister to readers through the characters and lessons you've given to me in *Heaven Can Wait*.

Thank you to Tate Publishing and all of the employees who helped to take this book from my heart to what you hold in your hands. A special thank you to my editor Meghan Gregg, who encouraged me to reach deep inside of myself and make what I thought was already good to be even better. Nothing less than the best would do.

Thank you to my father, Charles E. Jessamy Jr., for endless parental guidance and life lessons. For being larger than life and for never letting me forget what responsibility and accountability mean as the oldest sibling. But most of all, you never let me quit on my dreams.

Thank you to my mother, M. Denise Jessamy, who has always lived out her faith to the best of her ability for all of us to see. For the endless and selfless sacrafices that she makes, not out of duty but out of love. Hopefully she'll be able to carry the crowns that await her in Glory.

Thank you to my oldest, Christopher John. You've been an inspiration to me the moment you came onto the scene. Had it not been for you in my life, I would have given up many times over. I carry you in the deepest places in my heart and I'm so very proud of the man you've grown up to be.

Ceaira, for the countless times you've read the story, your ideas and words of encouragement shared, thank you. You, my only daughter, keep me in awe. The gifts and talents God has bestowed on you seem to be without limits, so the day you told me you were proud of me is a day that I'll cherish forever. God's love and light shine in and through you everywhere you go, don't ever let either one be distinguished; for without Christ, we are nothing.

Clifton, you may be the second to the youngest, but you posses great wisdom for a young man, almost as if you've been through all this before. You know how I tease that you're my old man in a young man's body, but I mean it as the greatest compliment. I cherish our talks and times of fun together. You'll make your mark in this world with the hand and favor of God, wait and see.

To my youngest, Channing, although you're a teenager now, you continue to view the world through childlike eyes and wonder. No thing is too great or too hard for you to achieve. Don't ever lose your joy and love of life; it's a gift from God. It may be those big brown eyes that melt people's hearts now, but someday soon it'll be your love for God that will turn people's hearts to Him.

Thank you especially to my husband Francis. I love to tell people how God brought you from another continent and me from another state to New York where our paths crossed many times before becoming friends and then later husband and wife. All of these years later, I still swoon over you and can't seem to ever tire of your company. You're one of the most hardest working, respected men that I know who loves his family without end. May God's favor, love, and peace forever fill your life.

And finally to all of you who will support me in this new "chapter" in my life, a heartfelt thank you. My hope is that this first book will touch you in a way that encourages your faith to rise to a new level. May God's continual blessings be manifested in your lives....

Forever grateful, Tiki C. Durand

Kristy's heart raced with excitement as she waited for the lights to be lit on the tree at Rockefeller Center. She looked at the different faces in the crowd gathered in the square, and she noticed people from every walk of life. A group of teenage friends laughing while they sipped their hot chocolate or lattes, couples smiling at one another with wide-eyed anticipation or holding hands, mothers with their children getting antsy as they waited in the cold December air. She was standing right next to the film crew from a local television station, but she hardly noticed them as they began to set up. Instead her attention was focused on a star shining brightly directly above the tree. It seemed to be dancing in the night sky as if it shared the joy that filled every part of her being. The tears welled up in her eyes, and she said a silent prayer of thanks to God. It was hard to believe that only a year ago she had given up on life, so much so that she had even made up her mind to take matters into her own hands and end it all one night. She began to think back to the events that had led up to what was almost her final hour.

Tiki Durand

———◆◆◆———

Kristy sat in church and listened to her pastor preach on standing on the promises of God for the umpteenth time. She rolled her eyes toward the ceiling and thought to herself, *I wouldn't have to keep standing if He would just answer my prayers.* She sighed as she looked at the empty seat next to her. Even though she had pleaded with Brian to come to church with her, he had refused. Once again he told her that he had to go into the city and work on yet another deadline that afternoon, and so he needed a few hours of extra sleep. This was now the fifth Sunday in a row. When she had asked him why he hadn't gone into the office on Saturday, he pulled the covers over his head and went back to sleep. So she got dressed and went to church alone, again.

Kristy Anne Marie Felix had been married to Brian for the last six years, and she knew him better than he knew himself. So she couldn't help noticing that something about him was very different lately. She had been so sure that once she told him they were going to be parents things would have gotten better. Instead he only seemed to have become more distant. It wasn't just the six-day workweeks with ridiculously long hours or his missing church for the last several weeks, that had her on edge; there were other things that had changed as well. Small things that only a wife as close to her husband as she was might notice. Like the "just because" calls that he would make to her three or four times a day had pretty much stopped. His appetite was gone and he was biting his nails, something he only did when he was either stressed out or anxious. He was

Heaven Can Wait

working more and sleeping less. Whenever she asked him if everything was okay, he'd get very agitated and tell her to stop worrying. Except no matter how hard she tried, she couldn't stop. The more she tried to figure it all out, the more frustrated she got. Brian was no stranger to working under the pressure of a deadline, so what was it about these last few that were altering his behavior so much? No, there had to be something else going on, something that Brian was keeping from her. She gently caressed her stomach, which was hardly noticeable yet, even though she was a couple of days shy of entering her fifth month of pregnancy, and tried very hard to focus on what Pastor McKnight was saying.

"God knows what you have need of before you can even ask for it. He has even already made the provisions for you."

"Amen," came from several of the congregants in the benches.

"Yeah, well, God, what I need is to know why my husband is straying away from both you and me." She complained under her breath as she reached angrily for her bag and walked out. By the time she reached her car, she was crying. She wanted desperately to call her Aunt Cynthia, but Kristy knew that her aunt was still in her own church service. Over the years her Aunt Cynthia had become the voice of reason in her head. She had raised Kristy after she took her in after her parents died in a train wreck when Kristy was just ten years old. At the time Kristy came to live with her, Cynthia had just turned thirty and was still unmarried, with no children of her own. Cynthia was Phylicia's younger sister by five years. But when the question came up concerning her sister's only child, she stepped up to the responsibility without hesitation. The Child Welfare Services would have had a problem with the arrangement, except for one thing: Cynthia was very wealthy.

As part of a high school curriculum, Cynthia had started interning on Wall Street when she was just a junior. She stayed with the company throughout her college education, continuing to observe and learn everything she could. The senior partner and her boss at the time, Frank Harris, was a very shrewd man. He had taken an instant liking to Cynthia, which could of had something to do with the fact that she reminded him of his granddaughter who lived out in Sedona, Arizona. They were about the same age and height. Both had beautiful sandy-brown hair and mesmerizing brown eyes. Cynthia had dimples, which he referred to as small craters, and Libby did not. Cynthia was a quick learner, and he began teaching her everything he knew over the two years she interned and on her summer breaks from college. When she graduated she was offered an executive position. Within three years she had exceeded the board's expectations so much, they offered her a partnership in the company. Eight years, an ulcer, hypertension, and an impressive financial portfolio later, Cynthia retired. After her sister's death, she flew out to Denver, packed up her niece and her belongings, and brought her to Westchester County in New York. She spent the rest of the year adjusting to being a guardian. Cynthia helped Kristy with her homework, school projects, and chaperoned class trips.

She even signed up to be a troop leader for the Girl Scouts. At the end of the year, Kristy's school had a carnival to help raise money for the following year's school trips. There were rides, games, food, and prizes. The PTA asked for volunteers to help out in various ways—setting up, ticket sales, donations, food preparation, and cleaning up. Cynthia offered to make handmade dolls and donate them to sell. It was something she learned to do in a core humanities designer class in college. She made ten cloth dolls with beautiful outfits and yarn hair to style. The day of the fair, the dolls sold out within an hour. She was in shock. Two women who ran a daycare center from the town approached her and asked if she would make more dolls for an arts and crafts show they were going to have over the summer. They exchanged cell phone numbers, and Cynthia promised to consider it. Over the next several months, there were more requests, so she did the only thing a woman in her position could do; a year later she opened her own doll boutique on Main Street.

Word about her shop spread fast, and business was good. It didn't hurt that Cynthia had some connections in advertising from when she had worked on Wall Street. She helped to make some of the AD agencies quite successful with her financial advice, and they were only too happy to help her promote her new business endeavor.

A few days after one Thanksgiving, an attractive-looking man with striking salt-and-pepper hair walked into her store. Despite the gray Cynthia didn't think he could be more than forty. It had been a windy day so his hair was a little disheveled, but he hadn't noticed. Cynthia did everything she could to suppress the urge to laugh when he approached the counter. It seemed he was looking for a birthday present for his niece, and someone from his church suggested that he visit her boutique store. Cynthia asked him a few routine questions about the little girl. It was her own technique of trying to match the child's personality with the right doll. After showing him a few selections, he made his choice and purchased the doll, a beautiful ballerina. As Cynthia wrapped the gift, he made idle chitchat about the usual pleasantries—the weather, the holiday season, the increasing price of gas. Cynthia would nod politely as she continued to wrap the gift. And a few moments later, he walked out of the store a little happier. Three weeks later he was back to purchase another doll for the same niece as a Christmas present. This time he introduced himself as Courtney Wade. He was the youth pastor at Hope Ministries—a church in town. Cynthia was a bit surprised by the fact that she was happy to see him again. She liked his smile and warm, friendly manner. His brown eyes danced as he talked about the children at the church. As she handed him the gift-wrapped package, he thanked her and headed toward the door. But instead of walking out like he did the last time, he stopped just before opening the door, turned around, and quite nervously invited her for a cup of coffee after she closed that evening. Of course she agreed. And at nine o'clock sharp, Pastor Courtney Wade was waiting by the door. Cynthia quickly turned the lights off, and as she took a step to open the door, she lost her balance and headed for the floor. The next thing she knew, she was in Courtney's arms, and what strong arms they were. He held her that way for what seemed to her like many moments, but at the same time, it also seemed as if time was standing still. She found her footing and thanked him as she stood up.

The coffee shop was empty and they found a place to sit next to the window immediately. Taking their seats across from one another, Courtney removed his coat and Cynthia noticed he was wearing a white turtleneck with a green sweatshirt over it. But it was what was written on the sweatshirt that caught her attention: Bethany College. When she asked him about it, he told her that Bethany was his alma mater. She extended her hand across the table as if to shake his and with a huge smile announced that she too was a graduate from Bethany. What were the odds? The school only had 900-1000 students each year. And if that wasn't enough of a coincidence, they had graduated only three years apart from one another. So when Courtney was a senior, Cynthia was a freshman. They talked about how they had both wound up at the school and then the conversation turned to their families. Cynthia asked about Courtney's niece and she told him about hers. Cynthia felt so comfortable in Courtney's company. They continued to talk long after they had emptied their coffee mugs. It wasn't long before they were meeting on a regular basis. Two months later Cynthia brought Kristy to Courtney's church for youth fellowship one Friday night. Kristy had enjoyed the service and asked if she could attend again the following week. An immediate bond formed between Courtney and Kristy, which came as no surprise to Cynthia; after all, he was experienced in dealing with children. Watching the two laugh and talk at ease melted Cynthia's heart, and she knew she was in trouble. By the summer they were planning a wedding. After the marriage Courtney became Uncle Courtney to Kristy, and he did his best to be a godly role model. Courtney loved to talk to Kristy about the Lord as he prepared dinner. It was their special time together. Kristy would sit on the bar stool at the island while Courtney cooked on the stove. The excitement on Kristy's face and the way she hung on to every word amazed Cynthia. He had such an anointing with children. Many "world topics" were discussed between the two during those times; homework, school projects, would the Yankees make it to the World Series one more time, which comic series was better (DC or Marvel), boxed macaroni and cheese or oven baked, Kristy's first crush, Jaime Correa, but more times than not it was surrounded by accounts from the Bible. One night as they talked, Courtney sensed God's presence in their midst. And that night he led Kristy into a prayer that would change her life forever, the prayer of Salvation.

Kristy sat in the church parking lot in her car with the engine running, not wanting to go home just yet. Instead she headed east on I-287 and drove to her job. She suddenly had a taste for Lorious's egg salad on whole wheat toast. Fifteen minutes later she pulled under the porte cochere of the Grandiose Hotel. Eric, her assistant manager, looked surprised when he saw her enter through the revolving doors. Kristy's low-heeled sandals echoed as she walked across the light-marble floor to the mahogany registration counter. Making an attempt to hide how she was feeling on the inside, she put a little pep in her step. Thankfully the lobby was relatively quiet, since it was Sunday and after the eleven o'clock check-out time, so her charade wasn't too hard to maintain.

"Kristy, what are you doing here on your day off?" He smiled cheerfully. Kristy tried to return his smile, but his question reached right to her heart and the effort seemed to drain her.

She patted her stomach and replied casually, "I'm here to see a man about a sandwich." Eric wasn't buying it, though. He could see right through her.

"What's the matter?" he questioned, as he stepped out from behind the desk. Immediately at his question, Kristy's eyes filled with tears, but she didn't cry. Eric fumbled in his back pocket and produced a handkerchief. The gesture made her smile. He never ceased to amaze her. How many twenty-three year olds carried handkerchiefs? She often joked with him that he was an old man trapped in a young man's body. But she didn't mind. He was very responsible and took great pride in his job and the responsibilities that went along with it. Eric had gone to college for hospitality and aspired to one day be a general manager. And although he had only been with the hotel for a little over three years, he and Kristy acted as if they had known each other all their lives. She often said he was the younger brother she never had.

"Nothing's wrong. I think my hormones are just out of whack. I got this whole pregnancy thing going on, you know."

"You're going to have to do better than that. You can't lie to save your life." Kristy turned on her heel and began to walk to the lounge. Eric followed step right beside her. Eric's six-foot-three height made her own of five-foot-five feel even shorter.

"Am I going to have to call Brian?" he teased innocently. But Kristy tensed up at the mention of her husband's name, and she knew that Eric had noticed. He gave her a piercing look as if he were trying to read her mind. She didn't respond but instead kept walking in silence while Eric waited patiently for Kristy to open up. One of the things he had learned about Kristy over the past years was she talked when she wanted to talk and kept quiet when she didn't. They sat down in a corner booth away from the few people who were dining. Kristy laid her head against the backing and let out a deep sigh.

In a whispered tone, she spoke the words to express what she had been feeling for weeks now, "I don't think Brian is very happy. I'm not sure yet if it has to do with the baby or something else."

"Kristy, that's ridiculous. You told me that he's wanted to have children with you ever since the beginning of your marriage. Maybe he's just a little nervous now that it's happening, and he is still getting used to the idea."

"It's more than that—" she started but was interrupted by their server, Julia.

"Hi, Kristy. Hi, Eric," she greeted them, but her eyes were fixated on Eric.

"Hi," they both answered in unison. She handed them menus all the while never once taking her eyes off of Eric.

"I don't need a menu, thanks. I would like an egg salad sandwich on whole wheat toast, please." The thought of the sandwich was making her mouth water. She could already taste the cilantro, dill, and red peppers that made Lorious's recipe her favorite.

"Sorry, Kristy. We are all out." Julia could see the disappointment on Kristy's face and quickly added, "We had a track team in here for lunch and, well, you know how they can eat." As if that would make Kristy feel any better.

"Oh, that's right. I forgot they were here this weekend. I just can't seem to catch a break today." She sighed. Eric cleared his throat and shot Julia his best smile.

"Why don't you be a gem and ask Lorious if he could do this for Kristy as a favor. I've heard that when a woman who is expecting doesn't get whatever she is craving, it marks the baby, or something like that."

"That's not true. It's just an old wives' tale." But it hardly mattered what Kristy said. Julia was already heading toward the kitchen. She stumbled once and quickly looked over her shoulder to see if Eric had noticed. Kristy couldn't help but to laugh.

"You really shouldn't tease Julia like that, Eric. It's quite obvious she has a thing for you."

"Never mind about that right now. What were you saying?"

"Eric, you're relentless." She shook her head and continued, "In all honesty, Brian was acting strange before he even knew I was pregnant. He's been working six-day workweeks for over three months now. He's irritable and barely sleeps. Sometimes I wonder which one of us is pregnant." She played with Eric's handkerchief to avoid looking at him.

"Have you tried asking him what's wrong instead of worrying yourself?"

"Well duh. Of course I have. But he always insists he's just under the pressure of yet another deadline." Her hazel-brown eyes began to tear up for the third time in less than an hour. "Maybe the real truth is that he doesn't love me anymore." The words didn't sound right to her, but what else could it be?

"Yeah, you're right," Eric said so agreeably that Kristy could have snapped her neck with how quickly she looked up at him.

"Excuse me?"

"I mean you're right about the fact that your hormones are out of whack. You're crazy if you think that Brian doesn't love you anymore. I've been around you two long enough to know that's just not possible." Out of the corner of her eye, she could see Julia heading back to their table. She had blonde, shoulder-length hair that was pulled back in a ponytail and swayed from left to right as she practically bounced to the table.

Kristy didn't dare tell Eric what she really feared was the reason. She didn't even believe it herself; but the thought kept nagging at her incessantly.

"Lorious is fixing that sandwich for you. Eric, can I get you something to drink while you wait?" There was no mistaking the cues; Julia did indeed have a thing for Eric.

"Any particular reason why you're not offering to take a food order for me?" He feigned a mock insult.

"I noticed you when you went to lunch around 12:30." She smiled brightly. Eric nodded in response and returned her smile.

"I'm fine, thanks. I have to get back to the desk anyway." Eric gently squeezed Kristy's hand. "I'll see you Tuesday, and stop overreacting." Kristy watched Eric as he walked away and wondered if he was right. Was she making too much of Brian's behavior? Was it really just the paranoia of a pregnant woman? "Dear Lord, please let me be wrong." She prayed under her breath, but that nagging ache inside told her that those feelings wouldn't be dismissed so easily.

———◆———

Lori Adams waited for the number-four bus, barely noticing the other people standing next to her. She felt sick. Her stomach was filled with butterflies, and her heart was pounding so fast she felt like she would pass out at any moment. She needed to sit down. *Where is the bus?* she thought silently. Almost as if the bus driver had heard her thoughts, the number-four bus turned the corner and pulled up directly in front of her. Lori stepped inside and paid her fare. She quickly spotted two empty seats and sat on the isle, placing her bag on the other seat. The last thing she wanted was for any one to sit down next to her. She needed to think. She needed to plan what to do next. As the bus rolled off, she gazed out the window as the city began to pass by. Despite the fact that it was a beautiful spring day in Yonkers with the trees in full bloom and the sun shining brightly, Lori had a dark cloud over her. Outside the people on the streets were walking to and fro, unaffected by the information that she'd just been given in the last hour. After today her life will never be the same again. Regardless of how bad she was feeling at the moment, the outside world was oblivious. Life was still carrying on. It had a funny way of doing that.

Brian sat at his desk with his head cradled in his hands. While he was sitting in the office in New York City, desperately trying to keep one of the company's largest accounts from pulling out, his partner was lying on a boat somewhere off the Keys, fishing. John Felix had no idea of the turmoil his brother was dealing with back home. He had every confidence in Brian's ability to run the family business. John was more of the "face" of the business. He considered his role to be more of the partner who handled public relations. He smiled and looked good for the client and attended fundraisers and networking events. John would gladly agree that Brian was the brains behind the scene, the backbone and heart of Higher Thoughts, the advertising company their father started forty five years ago. Not that Brian minded being there. He wasn't comfortable in the spotlight. But right now—at this moment—he desperately needed John. They were on the verge of losing everything. Just two days earlier, he got the call that Creative View, a very successful company that sells graphic design software, was looking to sign with Blazon Marketing, another advertising company uptown. If that happened, their company would be done. At the moment Creative View's account was the only thing keeping them above water. He didn't know what to do. He glanced at the picture of Kristy on his desk and reached for it. She was so beautiful, even more so now that she was carrying their child. He traced the outline of her auburn hair with his finger. His mind flashed back to the other night when he came home early to surprise her but instead found her asleep on a lounge chair on the deck. The sun was setting and casting a soft glow over her whole body. It was almost as if God Himself was blanketing her. She was radiant. He remembered that he was caught off guard at the sight of her. After six years of marriage, she still caused his heart to skip a beat. He hoped it would always be that way.

Brian wanted so badly to tell her what was going on. In the entire time of their marriage, they had never kept secrets from one another. That is, until now. At first he didn't tell her because he didn't think there was any cause for alarm. However, when things went from bad to worse, he knew it was time to talk. He had made up his mind to tell her right before leaving for John and

Veronica's house for the company's annual Labor Day cookout. Just as he mentioned to Kristy he needed to talk to her, she said she needed to talk to him, too, and asked if she could go first. Without waiting for him to respond, she announced with great enthusiasm, "We're going to have a baby!" She told him she had found out a few days earlier but thought it would be amusing to tell him on Labor Day. He didn't have the heart or the nerve to tell her the truth after that. The last thing he wanted, in her newfound condition, was for her to worry. He felt as if the black clouds had just opened up and began pouring rain all over him. When Kristy asked if he was happy about the news, he told her he was, of course, just taken by surprise. Deep inside he truly was happy, but the timing couldn't have been more wrong. Now, on top of all his other worries, he was going to be a father. And ever since that afternoon, he had been hearing those words in his head continuously. As much as he didn't want her to worry, he knew his recent behavior was giving her plenty cause to do that very thing. She knew him too well, and she had asked him on several occasions if everything was all right. Each time he had either lied, changed the subject, or acted like he hadn't even heard her. With each passing day, it became harder and harder to tell her the truth, and he didn't know how to tell her without causing her to get stressed. He kept thinking that if he could get the company back on track, maybe if he even found some new accounts to replace the ones that had left, everything would be fine, and he wouldn't have to upset her. But sitting in the office for the last few hours, reviewing things, it was becoming more evident to him that he could no longer keep this from her. So he'd come to the decision that tomorrow he'd talk to Kristy. He'd tell her everything and promise her that somehow, he'd make everything alright so she wouldn't worry. He just hoped he could convince her because over the last several weeks, he'd done everything he knew to do and things hadn't gotten any better and he was no longer sure himself. But right now, tonight, he only wanted a good night's sleep. Every part of his body ached, and instinctively he knew there was no rest in sight. Or at least not any time soon.

After leaving the hotel, Kristy decided she needed to shake the blue mood she was in. She knew that God is not the author of confusion but of peace; however, at the moment she didn't sense His presence near her. So she decided to go to the Westchester Mall and walk around. She had only been at the mall for a few minutes when as she passed the information desk she heard her name being yelled out from across the way. Kristy laughed, not loud enough for anyone else to hear though. Only one person could shout in a crowded mall and still be heard, and that was her Aunt Cynthia. In the next instant Kristy spotted her aunt near the pretzel stand and motioned with her hand that she was coming over. A smile formed on Kristy's face as she crossed over to meet her aunt. God was so funny; she had only thought about talking to her aunt just a little while ago and now here she was. She was sure her Heavenly Father had set this up. He was just so good like that.

"What are you doing here?" she asked, greeting her with a kiss on the cheek.

"I could ask you the same question. And where is Brian?" She looked around, but no sign of her nephew-in-law was in sight.

"He's at the office so I decided to do a little window shopping." Oddly, the desire she had had earlier to pour her heart out to her aunt had mysteriously disappeared now that the two were facing each other.

"Window shopping? Nonsense. I'm feeling very generous. Let's buy something for my little blessing." She rubbed Kristy's stomach and headed for the department store at the end of the mall. "You know, I had a feeling I was going to see you here."

"Really?" Kristy raised one eyebrow with disbelief.

"Yeah, I spotted you the moment you stepped out of the elevator. So what do we buy for a baby that's still four months away?" She headed to the nursery section. "We don't even know if it's a girl or a boy yet, do we?"

"No, Aunt Cynthia, we don't, and we are not going to find out either. If God wants me to know, He'll reveal it to me. Besides, even if I had wanted to ask Dr. Anderson at my last appointment, it was too early. And I don't go back for another three weeks since he'll be out of the office attending a conference." Kristy was feeling better already, just thinking about the baby. The life that was growing inside of her everyday was truly a miracle. She had been reading her medical journals and books on pregnancy month by month and one of them had said that by the second trimester, the baby could hear what was going on in the outside world. So at night Kristy would sit on the couch and read all of her favorite Bible scriptures, just like she used to do with her Uncle Courtney. She couldn't wait to be a mother. And being there with her aunt, standing in the middle of the newborn section was the first time she was shopping for baby stuff. It was exciting.

"What about this? It could be for a boy or a girl." Cynthia held up a beautiful yellow quilt of baby animals on Noah's Ark. Kristy immediately nodded her head in approval. Pleased that Kristy was in agreement, Cynthia felt she had a green light to continue.

"Well, we can't just get the quilt. We have to get the whole set." Cynthia had spotted the crib set and mobile on the next shelf and was already in the midst of reaching for it.

"But we don't even have a crib yet," Kristy protested.

"We can solve that." Cynthia had a dangerous look in her eyes. Kristy began to panic. She knew her aunt well enough to know what would be next. She had to stop her without offending her.

"That would be wonderful, Aunt Cynthia, but Brian and I really want to do that together." She was sure that was the truth even though they hadn't talked about it yet. Cynthia stopped in her tracks and looked at her niece.

"Oh, I'm sorry. I didn't mean to overstep my bounds. I'm just so happy about the baby." Her tone held a hint of disappointment.

"I know." Kristy hugged her. "I'll make a deal with you. After Brian and I pick out the crib, you and Uncle Courtney can come over and help us put it together."

"That's a deal. So you feel like a manicure?" Kristy laughed at both her aunt's quick recovery and her unpredictability before agreeing. Clearly happy again, Cynthia picked up the quilt, crib set, and mobile. When Kristy shook her head, Cynthia chided, "We'll just keep it in the shopping bag in the baby's room for now. Yeah, that works." Kristy kept shaking her head while her aunt ignored her and walked to the register.

Lori arrived at her home in the upper Bronx, walked through the door, and threw her jacket and purse on the beige suede sofa. She headed for the kitchen and poured herself a glass of water.

"Hey, I didn't hear you come in." Jimmy said as he entered the kitchen. A startled Lori dropped the glass on the floor and it broke, water spilled everywhere.

"Lori, what's the matter?"

"I didn't know you were home." Her voice was shaking.

"Sorry, babe. I didn't mean to scare you. I thought I'd surprise you and come home early. But you weren't here. Where'd you go?" He picked up the pieces of broken glass and tossed them into the garbage. Considering her day and the news she'd been given, she wasn't ready to face him. Not just yet.

"Nowhere. Just out." Her heart began to beat so hard that she wondered if somehow he could hear it. "It was such a pretty day, I just wanted to get some... some fresh air," she stammered. Jimmy looked at her with a puzzled expression as he reached for the paper towels off the role from the counter.

"Okay. I was just asking. This isn't an interrogation." He tried to joke, but his attempt failed. Lori wasn't in the mood. She was feeling too many emotions at the moment, and playful was not on the list.

"I'm going upstairs to lie down," she said abruptly and walked out of the kitchen then added, "And no, that's not an invitation for company."

"That's the thanks I get for coming home early?" he yelled up from the bottom of the stairs. Lori didn't bother to stop. "I'm trying Lori, and you keep pushing me away. What more can I do?" He sounded distressed.

"I didn't ask you to come home, so deal with it," she shouted as she slammed the door behind her.

Jimmy stood at the bottom of the stairs for a minute. He had to get through to Lori. But how? As it was, he was making all kinds of attempts to prove to her he'd changed. He thought about going into the bedroom and letting her know that he'd willingly go to counseling if she still wanted to. But he could still hear the echo of the door slamming in his ears and thought it best to give her space. He wondered what had her so on edge. Things had been strained between them but there seemed to be something more happening today.

A familiar desire began to creep up. Jimmy was thirsty. He swallowed hard and clenched his fist. He wasn't that man anymore—he'd been changed by the Love of Christ. He new the urge for a drink was because of what had just transpired between him and Lori. If only she'd just give him another chance. *Calm down*, he told himself. *Lord I need your help, please tell me what to do.* He prayed silently. Then from somewhere inside his heart, a passage from First Corinthians, chapter thirteen, which is known as the love chapter, came back to him. It said that Love is patient and kind and that it always hopes for the best and that it endures. In a matter of moments he made up his mind. He would not give up on Lori or their marriage. He'd do whatever was necessary to prove to her that he loved her. No matter how she responded, no matter what she said, he wouldn't stop until he won her back. *Love endures*, he thought again.

Lori sat on her window seat and pulled her legs up to her chest. He looked so hurt when she walked away, but it was too late. He had hurt her too deeply. No matter how much she still loved him, no matter how much she wanted to run into his arms and feel the warmth of his embrace, she had to protect herself from ever feeling such pain again. Lori's doubts outweighed her hopes at this point. Was she to believe now that all of a sudden because Jimmy supposedly found the Lord that he was really changed, and she was expected to act like all was forgiven? He wasn't thinking about God when he was out drinking with the guys from his job two and three times a week. He wasn't thinking about God on those weekend trips to Atlantic City, gambling away their money and lying about it afterward. And he wasn't thinking about God when he refused to go to counseling, even after she told him that if he didn't agree to go to save their marriage she would leave him. Was she to believe that a God capable of only good would even want Jimmy, who couldn't even honor the wedding vows he made to her, in a church no less, in front of all of their family and friends? But then again, why wouldn't God want Jimmy with all of his faults? After all, she still did, no matter how much she tried to deny it. And besides, wasn't that what salvation is all about, exchanging the life of a sinner with the life of a Holy Savior who suffered innocently for all the sins of the world?

Lori looked on at the people outside for the second time that day. All of them busy living their lives. But what was she going to do? Her head was beginning to hurt from all of the thinking, or maybe it was the worrying, she had been doing since leaving Dr. Anderson's office. Lori had been feeling ill for a few weeks. It didn't make a difference what she took; she hadn't been able to shake whatever was attacking her body. When she first called her doctor, who also happened to be her father's best friend, she was only experiencing an achy feeling. She thought it was the signs of the flu late in the season. No matter how much she rested, she was still fatigued though. She told him she wasn't running a fever, but a few times she had felt lightheaded. When he asked her if she might be pregnant, she emphatically told him no. Even though her period had been erratic and very light over the last few months, she was sure that wasn't even a possibility. For one, she was using the birth control patch, which, she told him, he should know since he prescribed them for her. And two, she and Jimmy's moments of intimacy had been few and far between. But before hanging up with her, he made her promise that if she didn't feel better in a few days to call his office and make an appointment to come up to Yonkers to see him. Lori halfheartedly agreed, but when the symptoms worsened, she called him at home instead. Being that it was Sunday, he instructed her to meet him at the hospital where he was affiliated. She tried to push it off until Tuesday, but he had insisted. Cursing herself for being so paranoid, she got showered and dressed and caught the bus. Of all weekends to have dropped her car off for maintenance repairs and detailing, why did it have to be that one? She had arranged to pick up her car on Monday since the service station was closed on Sundays, and she hadn't thought she'd need it until then. After only an hour of testing, Dr. Anderson had come back with the results. "*Against all obstacles, life has a way of triumphing,*" he told her. Lori was indeed pregnant. Thirteen weeks to be exact.

She needed time to take in everything. Her being pregnant and Jimmy's newfound Christianity—was it somehow tied together? She ran her fingers through her short, curly, jet-black hair. "Is this some kind of cruel joke?" she asked, looking up at the ceiling, half expecting an answer. When none came, she took out the prescription Dr. Anderson wrote out for her. It was for prenatal pills with an added dose of iron. He had also found that Lori was slightly anemic. In about twenty-seven more weeks, she would be a mother, which would also mean that Jimmy would be a father. She knew there was no way she could leave him if she told him. As it was, he'd been making an effort of coming straight home after his shifts from work. He was a utility worker for Easy Share Power Co. That was, in fact, how they had met.

Shortly after Lori had moved into her townhouse, there was a very bad thunderstorm. She lost power for two days. Jimmy was the worker who came to restore her service. Two years later, they were married, and eighteen months past that, she was contemplating ending their marriage. She turned away from her window and looked at their queen-sized bed. Maybe if she took a nap she would feel better. Yes, she decided, sleep is what she needed. *Sleep has a way of working wonders for the mind,* she thought silently, crawling under the covers.

Brian walked into the house and could immediately hear Kristy singing along to one of her favorite Christian CDs in the kitchen. Suddenly he felt a different pang of guilt. He'd skipped church for yet another Sunday. He mentally added that to the growing list of recent personal short falls. He entered the kitchen, and sure enough, there was Kristy dancing around the stove. Her hair was in a messy ponytail that swayed from side to side as she moved to the upbeat song. She was wearing his black T-shirt that was way too long for her and hung below her waist and a pair of black stretch pants. He looked down at her feet, barefoot and manicured. In the back of his mind the reference, barefoot and pregnant, surfaced. Was it his imagination, or was she getting more beautiful each day?

"Something smells good." He said with a genuine voice.

"Thanks," she replied.

He set his briefcase down near the table and moved in close behind her at the stove. He eyed the fresh string beans steaming in one pot and rice pilaf in the other one. He was pretty sure he smelled Kristy's tasty roast pork loin in the oven. He switched on the oven light and confirmed his suspicion. His taste buds danced as he imagined the flavor of her rosemary sauce on the roast.

"You must have had a really good day." He looked down at her.

"I wasn't expecting you so early. For the last few weeks, you haven't come home at all for Sunday dinner." She avoided making eye contact. He seemed to be in a good mood but Kristy couldn't be sure which facet of Brian's personality she was dealing with yet.

"I...um..."—he cleared his throat, realizing that Kristy's defenses were up— "I decided to call it a day. John is still away, and I couldn't think anymore." What he really wanted to say was that he missed her and wanted to come home and hold her close. But the words wouldn't come out.

"What about your deadline? Aren't you concerned about it, or was that just an excuse?" The words rushed out and sounded harsh in her own ears. She hadn't meant to say it quite like that, but there was no taking it back.

The words clipped at Brian, causing his defenses to rise as well. "An excuse, an excuse for what?" What was Kristy accusing him of, he wondered? She turned and finally looked up at him. Their eyes locked together for a brief moment. He could see the pain, the pain he knew he'd put there.

"For not coming to church, for getting away from me, or for not talking about what's wrong with you lately. Take your pick." The lump in her throat ached. She felt like crying, but she willed herself not to.

"Kristy, for the love of God—"

"Do you even know who God is anymore?" she interrupted. Brian sighed. *Just tell her. Right now. Tell her*, he said to himself. But he looked deeper into her eyes and again the words were stuck in his throat.

Catching him off guard, Kristy asked, "Is there someone else, Brian? Is that why you've been so distant? And now that I'm pregnant, you're worried that you'll have to choose between her and me and the baby?" A look of horror struck Brian's face. How could she even think such a thing? He knew he had been remote lately, but how did she arrive at that conclusion? Didn't she know him better than that? The guilt he felt earlier turned into insult. Whatever window of opportunity he had of telling her the truth had just closed.

"Maybe if you would stop harassing me every other minute I would have a reason for wanting to be here." His pride was hurt and he didn't bother to mask the anger in his voice. For the last few weeks he'd practically been killing himself trying to do everything he could to save the company his father left to him and

John, which would ultimately provide a better life for his family as well. How dare Kristy accuse him of this. He didn't deserve it. Brian reached for his briefcase and did the only thing he felt he could do at the moment: he stormed right out of the front door.

Kristy stood there and watched in disbelief as her husband left her in the middle of the kitchen. Not only was she upset over their argument but more than that, Brian had not denied a thing. The air around her suddenly felt thick and panic gripped her heart. She slid down the side of her wall, the tears flowing freely now.

She began to pray out loud. "What am I going to do, Lord? I don't want to raise this child on my own. You knew what he was doing, and you allowed me to get pregnant. I trust you, but why would you do that? Why, Lord?" She sobbed for several minutes, and then she felt the presence of God stirring around her.

She heard in her spirit, *Kristy, if you trust me, you wouldn't question me. Stand on my Word, and pray for your marriage and your child. Lean not to your own understanding. My strength is made perfect in your weakness.*

Only, Kristy didn't feel like praying. Her emotions were in control. She felt like crying as she imagined Brian running from their home into the arms of the other woman, the woman who was breaking up their marriage.

Brian walked to his car, not even knowing where he was going. He was hurt, angry, and—most of all—tired. He really wanted to go back inside and apologize to his wife. But he wasn't brave enough to see that look on her face again. He also lacked the energy for another confrontation. There was a distance that kept growing between the two of them. He didn't deny it was his fault, but he didn't seem to be able to close the gap. His thoughts turned to John, and for the first time since they were children, Brian wished, like most twins do from time-to-time, they could switch places. John, Brian's older fraternal twin by twelve minutes, always seemed to know how to handle conflict. He was the epitome of the cliché, smooth, calm, and collected. In high school he was the captain of the debate team, and rightfully so. His confident business tactics made him a good contract negotiator and deal closer. But there was one person to Brian's knowledge that he was never able to dazzle, and that was Kristy. Brian reached for his cell phone, flipped it open, and spoke John's name into the speaker. Immediately the phone began to ring.

"Hello?"

"John, it's me, Brian. Listen. I don't mean to bother you while you're tanning in Florida, but exactly when do you think you'll be back in New York?" There was no mistaking the sarcasm in Brian's voice, not that he was making an effort to conceal it. He was too tired for that.

"What's wrong?" John asked, sounding alarmed.

"This is not exactly how I wanted to tell you, but we might be looking for jobs soon. I've been killing myself trying to save this company, and as if that's not bad enough, Kristy and I are having problems because of it."

"Hold on. Back it up just a minute. One thing at a time. Exactly what is going on?" Brian couldn't tell if his brother was concerned or annoyed.

"I mean we've lost all of D'Lights accounts, and Creative View might be next. And if Virgil decides to leave, simply put, we're done."

"Virg can't go anywhere. He signed a three-year contract, and it's only been two."

"Yeah, well, their lawyers found a loop hole!" Brian was almost yelling now. Relaying everything to John on the phone was fueling Brian's temper even more. None of this made any sense. Something wasn't right but Brian couldn't place his finger on it. It had been nagging at him, like a picture that he couldn't quite make out because it was out of focus.

"Calm down. Getting excited isn't going to solve—"

"John you don't understand!" Brian cut him off. "My marriage is suffering. Kristy thinks I'm having an affair and…and…" He dropped the phone to his side for a moment to take a deep breath. Hearing for himself those last words pierced his heart. Tears rolled down his cheek, and he realized his hands were trembling.

"Brian, are you still there?"

Brian brought the phone back to his ear and answered, "Yes, John, I'm still here."

"Why in God's name would Kristy think you are having an affair?"

"Because I can't seem to tell her that we are in serious jeopardy of losing Higher Thoughts. And with the baby on the way, formula, diapers, daycare expenses for when Kristy goes back to work, not to mention medical costs and, and…"

"Brian, don't start getting carried away. Where are you anyway? It sounds like you're outside." Brian looked at his house, a beautiful, custom colonial with a stone front, three bedrooms, and two bathrooms. Maybe he shouldn't have been so quick to leave. He could have easily stayed in one of the spare rooms. "I walked out on Kristy after she accused me of having an affair. I still can't believe she could ever think that of me. How could she think that, John?" John was getting very nervous on the other end. His brother was rambling and sounded very distressed. He needed to talk some sense into Brian.

"Listen to me. You need to go back, and tell Kristy the truth. If you walked out and didn't explain things, she probably is really convinced that you're sleeping around." In his mad dash, Brian hadn't had time to consider that. His world had just gone from bad to worse.

"I can't. I can't go in there, John. You didn't see the look in her eyes. I just need some time to work things out." He sucked in his breath and let it out slowly before continuing, "John, when are you coming home?"

"I'll catch a flight out tomorrow. Brian, I still think you should go talk to Kristy."

"Tomorrow. I'll talk to her tomorrow after she calms down." He vowed.

"Where are going to go tonight? And what is she going to think when you don't come home? Are you thinking this out, Brian? You're not helping the matter." John could tell he wasn't getting through to his brother.

"Tomorrow, John. You'll come home, we'll figure things out together, and then I can face my wife and make it all up to her. I promise." Brian's words were barely a whisper, the fight that was there just but a moment ago, now gone.

John didn't speak for a few seconds. He didn't want to contribute to Brian and Kristy's fight but he also knew that his brother was stubborn and his mind was made up.

"You win. The house is empty. Go on by, and I'll see you tomorrow. I will try to get the first flight out."

"Thanks, John."

"See you tomorrow." John closed his phone and looked at Veronica, who had been standing in the doorway listening.

"We've got to pack and fly home. There's trouble on the horizon."

Lori woke up to find that it was morning. She climbed out of bed and rushed to the bathroom. She splashed some cold water on her face to fight off the wave of nausea she was feeling. But the hot, watery saliva was already forming in her mouth. She began to inhale and exhale repeatedly until she felt it pass. She brushed her teeth and turned on the shower all the while still trying to come to terms with the fact that she was going to be a mom. A few moments later, she stepped out and headed back into her room to get dressed. She wondered how long it would be before she started to feel better. Dr. Anderson told her that most women only experience morning sickness for the first trimester or so. She hoped he was right and that she would be one of them. As she pulled her sweater over her head, she noticed a vase filled with fresh yellow tulips next to her nightstand. She didn't remember them being there when she woke up, but then again she was busy rushing to the bathroom at the time. She loved tulips, and Jimmy knew it. She couldn't help but to smile. For weeks he'd been trying, reaching out on several occasions to reconnect with her. So many times she'd almost given in, like the night she came home from work and found that Jimmy had cleaned the entire house, washed all the clothes and cooked dinner. They had eaten by candlelight and afterwards watched a Christmas movie in the den. It had seemed like old times and when Jimmy kissed her that night, she didn't resist his advances. Now, three months later she was pregnant. She had a quick glimpse of the two of them looking down into the crib where their baby was sleeping. Would that ever be a reality? Why was she even allowing herself to hope? Her mini daydream was interrupted by the ringing of the telephone. It was the dealership letting her know that her car was ready. She finished getting dressed and caught a cab, picked up her car, and drove into work at Chips with Bytes Electronics. She had been with the company since it started six years ago. Her first position with the company was one as a sales representative, and then within just four years, she managed to work her way up to director of communications. She was proud of her accomplishments with the company, because she had worked hard to get to where she was. Several times she was bypassed by other executives that had more experience or knowledge.

All opportunities were fair and impartial, regardless of the fact that the founder and CEO was her father. Lori's father was an engineering graduate with a brilliant mind, both in business and technology. He worked for years at one of the top technology companies in the United States. Lori's mother finally convinced him to go into business for himself. In the first two years, when most companies were only breaking even, he had tripled his profits. He opened another office in the tri-state area, and eight years later, he had fifteen more locations throughout the country, even as far as California. Anyone who worked for Howard Klein had to jump through hoops to impress him, including his only daughter.

Lori walked passed her assistant, Rose, who was talking on the phone. By the smile she had on her face and the operator voice she was using, Lori could tell she was speaking to a customer. Rose looked up, and her smile got suspiciously bigger as Lori headed into her office. To Lori's surprise there was another bouquet of tulips on her desk. These were deep purple, pink, and white. She wondered where Jimmy had found tulips out of season. They were gorgeous. There was a card next to them. Lori opened the envelope and read the note.

Lori,

We need to talk. Please give our marriage one more chance. Dinner tonight at Luigi's. Eight O'clock. I love you.

James

Again, the hope of what could be resurfaced. The image she had seen earlier that morning came flooding back to her. She was stirred with emotions and she knew deep down what she wanted: she wanted Jimmy, her, and the baby to be a family. Suddenly she found herself doing something she hadn't done in years: sincerely praying to God. Lori couldn't pinpoint the exact moment when it happened, but she was feeling better, better than she had felt in a long time, emotionally and physically. "Who said prayer doesn't work?" she asked aloud to the empty office and picked up the phone to call her first of many clients for the day.

John and Veronica's plane landed at Westchester County Airport shortly after 9:30 a.m. Their driver, Ben, was waiting for them at the baggage claim. Fifteen minutes later they were pulling up in front of their home in Purchase. Brian's car was parked in their driveway, indicating he was still there. John asked Veronica if he could have some privacy with his brother when they got inside, and she willingly agreed.

Brian was sitting in the over-sized family room on the sofa. The news was on, but he was not paying attention to it. Instead he was staring out the window almost as if he were in a trance. John walked over and gently squeezed Brian's shoulder. Brian came back to reality, and instantly there was a look of relief to see John standing over him.

"I feel like such a fool."

"Yeah, we've all done things that make us feel like that from time to time."

"Veronica must hate me. I'm sorry, John."

"No, Veronica doesn't hate you, and I'm not the one you should be apologizing to. Have you talked to Kristy yet?" Brian ran his hand through his hair and sighed deeply.

"I tried to call her earlier this morning at the house, but she didn't answer. Then I tried her cell phone, and I just kept getting her voicemail. I guess she is still upset. What a mess."

"Why didn't you tell me about this before I left for Florida? I would have never gone." John kept his tone gentle, non-confrontational. He didn't want to upset Brian any more than he already was. He looked at his brother and could see the lines under his eyes. He could tell Brian hadn't slept and John's heart ached for him.

"I just kept thinking things would be okay, until Creative View called Tuesday and said they were reconsidering renewing their contract after receiving a tip that we had lost a couple of our other big accounts, and it was rumored we were going under."

"I called Taryn early this morning and got her up to speed on what's going on. She's actually in the office now reading their contract as well as D'Light's. She wants to know what loophole they found. What is our current assessment now that D'Light is gone?" John was partially afraid to ask.

"We are $1,750,000 in the red without them. And if Creative View doesn't renew, we're done. I thought that we could solicit some new accounts, but no body seems to be taking our calls. Marcus was visiting companies all week without any success. It's as if someone is purposely sabotaging us." Brian stood up and threw his hands up in the air.

"Okay, for now let's let Taryn and Steve go over the paperwork. I'm going to head into the office in another hour or two and make some phone calls myself. I want you to go home and talk this whole thing out with Kristy. She needs to know the truth, and I don't think you're giving her enough credit. She is not as fragile as you think." Brian shot John an angry look.

"Don't you think I know my own wife? Under ordinary circumstances, yes, she can handle this, but pregnant women are fragile."

"Brian, calm down. All I'm saying is that you've tried to keep this from her to protect her condition, and look what has happened. Would you rather let her believe that you're going to leave her and the baby for another woman?".

"No," Brian's shoulder's slumped as he answered quietly.

"Then go home, and talk to your wife," John urged one more time. "You've carried enough of the weight lately. I'll take it from here. Once you've worked everything out, come back to the office, but not before then. Understand?" John was using his older-brother, authoritative voice.

Defeated, Brian agreed. John hugged his brother and assured him that they would get through the ordeal together. Moments later, Brian was in his SUV, heading home. He attempted to reach Kristy again at home first and then on her cell phone. The results were still the same. He pulled up in front of the house. Kristy's car wasn't parked on the street. He opened the door and headed up the stairs toward their bedroom. He wasn't prepared to deal with what he found when he opened the bedroom door. Kristy's closet doors were open, and the once-filled space was practically empty. He walked over to her dresser and opened the drawers. Also empty. Kristy was gone.

———◆◆◆———

Cynthia quietly peeked in on her niece. She was upstairs in her old room, sleeping soundly. It had been an emotional night from the time Kristy showed up on their doorstep at ten-fifteen, carrying her luggage and crying uncontrollably. It took about half an hour to even get her to calm down long enough to make sense of what she was saying. Cynthia flashed back to the scene. Just as Kristy finished announcing that Brian was having an affair, she collapsed into her uncle's arms. Cynthia immediately headed for the phone to call Brian's cell phone, but Kristy begged her not to. She asked if she could stay with them until she figured out what to do next. Of course they both agreed, but none of it made any sense. Why would Brian do such a thing? It just wasn't in his character; he adored Kristy from the first day they'd met. And why now? Why would he wait until he and Kristy were expecting their first child? No, Cynthia was convinced there had to be a mistake, some reasonable explanation as to what was happening. She and Courtney both got on their knees together and prayed before they climbed into bed. She remembered having terrible dreams all night. About 5:00 a.m., she got up and headed downstairs to pray again. The words to one of her favorite songs were playing in her head: Just a little talk with Jesus makes it all right. But as she walked by Kristy's room, she could hear her niece still crying softly. It hurt Cynthia deeply to know Kristy was suffering. She had to do something; she just wasn't sure what.

John walked into his office to find Taryn behind his desk with a very unhappy look on her face. She was so intent that she hadn't even noticed that he had just entered the room. He stood in the doorway for a moment, just to observe her. She was flipping page after page of a thick file with one hand and furiously tapping a gold Monte Blanc pen in the other. He had to smirk at the sight, even though Taryn was nothing to laugh at. She was barely twenty-six, but because of her ambition, she was a much-respected lawyer. And to prove how respected she was, she charged $325 an hour for her services. Both John and Brian had tried repeatedly to get her on their staff full time, but she always teased that they couldn't afford her. She had majored in business law at Columbia University, and her specialty was in drafting contracts and grants. She was an independent lawyer and worth every penny of her time. The fact that she looked so agitated should have made John nervous, but it didn't. He cleared his throat. Taryn looked up, not bothering to conceal her concern, which was growing by the minute.

"It doesn't look good at all, John. This contract is ironclad. When was this clause added that mentions if at anytime the client begins to doubt the confidence of the company, they can cancel their contract, and all other clauses will become null and void?" There was no mistaking the anger in her question.

"Justin's son, Virgil, wouldn't sign the contract without the addendum. We figured we'd been doing business with his dad from the beginning and that he wouldn't dare do anything like this. We allowed it just to appease his conscience. But I guess since his father passed away last month, the wheels in his head started turning. But it still doesn't make any sense." He offered the explanation but considering their current situation, it seemed weak. Although he didn't know Virgil as well as he knew Virgil's father, Justin, the suddenness of this all seemed unlike him. John had a suspicious feeling that something more was going on, something he hoped could be revealed before things got any worse.

"No, it doesn't," Taryn agreed. "It's just seems too abrupt." She tossed her shoulder length brown hair over her right shoulder and then leaned back in his Executive leather chair. He'd seen this gesture before and knew the wheels in her head were turning. John figured he better fill her in on everything and decided it was best to not hold anything back. He took a depth breath before speaking his next words, "Well, I'm glad you're sitting down, because I don't know if Brian has mentioned that D'Light didn't renew their contract.

And we've lost two other smaller accounts. It seems as though they received a tip that we've lost a few clients and it's caused some concerns."

"What!" Taryn leaned forward and slammed her hand on the oak desk that had once belonged to John and Brian's father. She stood up and walked around to face John, folding her arms as she walked. "I don't like this at all. Not one bit. Something doesn't sound right. If I didn't know any better, I'd think someone was trying to sabotage Higher Thoughts."

"I've been thinking the same thing since last night. But who? How?"

She already had a thought and without any hesitation she asked, "With your permission, I'd like to hire my brother-in-law, Phil, to look into this."

"Let me talk with Brian first, but I don't think he'll object." John trusted Taryn's instincts and knew her brother-in-law was a well-respected private investigator. It couldn't hurt to have him dig around a bit and he was sure Brian would agree to it as well. Taryn nodded her head and walked over to phone and called Renee, John's assistant, and asked her to get her D'Light's file along with the other two companies that John had said left: Morry's Inc and Healthy Start Fitness.

"Call me once you've talked to Brian. I don't want to waste anymore time here." She ordered, sitting back down behind the desk.

"Neither do I," John concurred and walked out of the office. He had gotten as far as the water cooler in the reception area before he realized that he had just walked out of his own office, leaving Taryn in control of the room. He laughed at himself and continued on toward Brian's office. Taryn was definitely worth her weight in gold.

As soon as Renee handed Taryn the files she had requested, she left the office closing the door quietly behind her. If Taryn hadn't been so cautiously overlooking the papers laid out on the desk, she may have noticed the beads of perspiration on Renee's head. When she was sure no one else was around, Renee reached for her cell phone and dialed the number she now knew by memory.

"This better be good, I'm in the middle of a meeting." The voice on the other line spouted.

"Sorry to bother you but I thought you'd like to know they're starting to make the connections. They are reviewing all four companies contracts and it's only a matter of time before they find something. Taryn's smart, very smart." Renee couldn't hide the anxiety in her voice. She wished with all of her heart she could go back in time and change her decision to get involved with this. Despite everything, she really liked her job and her boss.

"Is that so? Well, no matter, we have Higher Thoughts just about where we want them." And without any warning, the call was ended.

All day Lori had been unable to concentrate. Her mind jumped from dinner with Jimmy, to wondering what she was going to wear, to imaging how she would tell him she was pregnant, and then to contemplating on whether she would even tell him at all. She had done more work in her mind than she had in the office all morning. Finally at about 3:15 p.m., she walked toward her dad's office and stopped to speak to his executive assistant. Priscilla looked up from her computer and smiled broadly. Lori noticed that Priscilla wasn't wearing her thick, black, bifocal glasses. "Priscilla, are you wearing contacts?" Lori asked, returning her smile.

"No, I had lasik surgery last week. It's amazing how clearly I can see everything."

"Well, you look even prettier. I give you a lot of credit. I think I'd be too scared to do anything like that. I won't even wear contacts. The thought of sticking those in my eyes,"—a shiver went through her whole body—"freaks me out." Priscilla laughed lightly.

"Your dad's inside, but he has a conference call in about twenty minutes." She motioned for Lori to go on in as she reached to pick up an incoming call.

"Thanks, Priscilla," she called back over her shoulder and walked into her dad's office and closed the door quietly behind her. Howard Klein peered up through his wire-brim glasses and met his daughter's gaze. At first Lori didn't move. All of a sudden she wasn't sure what to do.

"What's up?" he asked, noticing that Lori was still clutching the doorknob.

"Dad, I know how you don't like to let personal issues interfere with work, but,"—she stopped and suppressed the sudden urge to cry—"but I can't wait." A little concerned, Howard was now standing up behind his desk.

"Lori, what's the matter?" He removed his glasses and set them down on his large, cherry-oak desk. Lori knew from past childhood experience that gesture meant she had his undivided attention. There was no turning back now.

"Jimmy and I," her hands were sweaty and the air in the room seemed to have grown thick. "Jimmy and I have been having some problems." She managed to say.

"Yes, I know. Your mother has mentioned some things to me every now and then, but I never questioned you about it. I figured you would come to me if you needed to."

"You're always right, aren't you, Dad." He thought Lori was just trying to be flattering, but the look in her eyes showed something else. Her entire life Lori had been Daddy's little girl. Her father was her hero. They were as close as any father and daughter could be. When she was younger they'd spent almost every Sunday afternoon watching old black and white movies with a big bowl of popcorn. Abbott and Costello films were their favorites. They shared so many other interests, swimming, golf, their love for fine art. They even had the same taste in cuisine, middle Eastern being their top choice. Her mother often joked that she was the third wheel in the family.

Right now she was relying on the fact that he'd never once steered her wrong and she was hoping he could give her some direction. He walked around to the front of his desk and sat on the edge. He knew whatever it was, it was serious.

"Tell me what's wrong, honey." He motioned for her to move away from the door and take a seat in front of where he was sitting.

"As early as just yesterday morning, I was seriously thinking about coming home for a little while." She paused and then added, "That was until I came back from Dr. Anderson's." Howard Klein, clearly confused by his daughter's statement, frowned his face and then raised his eyebrows as the implications of her unspoken words sunk in.

"How far along are you?"

"I only took the pregnancy test so if his calculations are correct, I just ended my third month."

"And how did Jimmy take the news?"

"Well, that's what I wanted to talk to you about. I haven't told him. I thought we were on our way to a separation, and now this."

"Lori, was separation a mutual agreement?" Even though Lori was a grown woman, married, and about to have a child, she was still a little fearful of her father. She bit her lower lip and stalled for a few seconds before she spoke again. "No, just my idea. I'm so confused, Dad. First he was so wonderful, then he started gambling and hanging out at the bar, and now he's in the church, asking me to give our marriage another chance." She threw her head in her hands. Howard reached for his daughter's hand and lifted her chin with his finger.

"Lori, if he's trying to work it out, how can you still be confused. The answer is clear. You're pregnant, and every child needs both a mother and a father. Besides, you didn't get this way by yourself, obviously you still want to be in this marriage. Talk to your husband. Make him a special dinner, and tell him he's going to be a daddy." He smiled at her. The words came so confidently from him, no questions, doubts or hesitations. Was he right? She wondered. She rolled it over for a moment, her father waiting patiently and then she said,

"He actually invited me to dinner tonight to talk," allowing a smile to surface as well.

"See, that should tell you something. No man makes this much effort if he isn't serious about his commitments. He got a little crazy, but he's over it. He's never beat you or cheated on you. Listen," he held her hand a little tighter, "we've all been there. And I know I probably shouldn't say anything, but he came to see your mom and me just last night and apologized to us for not cherishing and realizing what a gift from God he has in you."

"What? Dad, why didn't you tell me that earlier?" Without thinking about it, Lori jerked her hand out from her father's. This was big. Jimmy, the Jimmy she knew would never do anything like that. What an act of humility.

"I told him we wouldn't say a word. But I think he would understand, considering what you've just told me." Lori stood up and threw her arms around her father.

"Congratulations, honey." He kissed his only daughter's cheek. As he watched her leave his office smiling, he wiped a tear from his own eye. The grey skies out-

Heaven Can Wait

side had just become a lot brighter, he was going to be a grandfather.

———◆◆———

Brian dialed Kristy's number again. He had lost count of how many times he had already tried. The result was the same as it had been each time before: unsuccessful. He was pretty sure he knew where she was. But did he have the courage to call? At this point he didn't have much of a choice; he needed to talk to Kristy. If he thought he'd been on edge before, coming home and finding her things gone had taken him right over. Why had he allowed things to get to this point? Shame and regret tugged at his heart and he hated how it felt. Looking back on it all, it had been a mistake to keep everything from Kristy. In his core he knew Kristy would have been able to handle it and if he had to be honest with himself, he also knew why he'd kept everything from her and from John. Pride; his own stupid, selfish pride. What did the Bible say about pride? It comes before the fall. And he couldn't agree more. But he had to try and make things right. He couldn't let things go any further. No way was he going to lose his wife and child over his stupidity. He just prayed it wasn't too late and that she'd find it in her heart to forgive him and come back home. Just as he was about to dial Courtney and Cynthia's home, his cell phone rang.

"Hello," he answered.

"It's me, John." Brian rolled his eyes, shaking his head. Of course he recognized his brother's voice; they were twins after all, not to mention his number came up on the caller ID. "It looks as if the loophole is legit. Remember Virgil had to make a big stink about not signing the contract unless he could make that one revision? Well, that's how he won out."

"Are you kidding me?" Brian ran his fingers through his hair—a gesture he only did when he was stressed, which lately was way too often.

"I was thinking that this all seems like too much of a coincidence. I mean, how did Virgil find out about D'Light leaving us anyway? Virgil and Wendy don't even know each other. Do they?"

"No." Brian was trying to recall any connections. "No, they don't."

"Well, Taryn wants to hire her brother-in-law to do some investigating. Someone's up to something, and I don't like it."

"At least we're not going down without a fight."

"We're sure not." John sighed and then added, "Speaking of fights, have you and Kristy talked yet?"

"She won't return any of my calls. I swear that woman is so stubborn."

"You know she is probably at her aunt's house. Why don't you just go on over there?"

"Yeah, I know you're right. But I don't know what she may have told them. And if I walk in there, and they look at me like I'm guilty, I...I don't think I can handle that, John."

"Brian, are you even thinking straight? You make it sound like you're guilty of what Kristy's accused you of. Just go on over there, and tell her the truth. Tell all of them. Who cares, as long as it's out in the open?

This isn't worth losing your wife over, or even worse, your child." John hated to be so direct, but he couldn't understand why Brian was dragging this whole mess out. And it was a mess.

"I'll call first just to be on the safe side."

"Your life, your choice." John put the receiver down and studied the photo of Kristy on Brian's desk. "God, it's all in your hands now," he spoke out loud.

———◆———

"Hi, Courtney. It's me, Brian." *Now I'm sounding as dumb as John.* He scolded himself silently.

"Don't you think I recognize your voice after all of these years?" he gently teased. "I know you're looking for Kristy, aren't you?"

"Oh, then she is there. Thank God." The tight knot in his stomach eased a bit. Even though he already had suspected as much, it still was a relief to have it confirmed.

"She's resting right now in her old bedroom. Why don't you come on by so the two of you can talk?" he suggested.

"I don't want to impose on you and Cynthia. Do you think she'll mind?"

"Cynthia or Kristy?" he teased again. But it went right over Brian's head.

"Both, actually."

"Well, between you, me, and the lamppost, Cynthia said Kristy mentioned that she couldn't believe you didn't come looking for her last night. Then she came to the conclusion that you must have stayed out all night."

"I did. But I was at John's house until this morning. I promise." He could feel his heartbeat begin to quicken.

"Brian, I believe you. Whatever is going on between you and Kristy, I have every bit of faith that you two will work it out. Come on by, son." Brian agreed and said he was on his way. Knowing that Courtney believed him and that he wasn't angry put Brian slightly at ease [somewhat]. Brian figured if he had Courtney on his side, Kristy might be likely to forgive him as well. She usually followed her uncle's lead. Feeling better, Brian decided to take a quick shower and shave before heading over to see Kristy. He'd wear the sweater she had gotten him for Christmas, along with her favorite cologne. Couldn't hurt to make himself irresistible while he begged her forgiveness. Might as well stop off and buy a box of her favorite chocolates, too. A smile tugged at his mouth at the thought. It was the first smile he could remember in a long time...

Courtney walked into Kristy's room and found her sitting up on the bed. She was clutching her pillow to her chest like she did whenever she was upset. His heart ached for her and he wished he could embrace her in a hug and chase all of her fears away, just like when she was a little girl. Only back then it was so much easier to fix whatever was ailing her; a loose tooth, bad dream, disagreement with a friend. No, this was so far beyond any of that, but he knew that when things were not within his control to fix, he served a God who with all things, it was possible. This is who he had to place his faith in now.

He let her know that Brian was on his way and that he wanted to talk. Knowing what Kristy had been thinking he thought it best to mention that Brian had slept all night at John's house and didn't realize that she wasn't home until this morning. Kristy looked a little bit comforted by the news and thanked her uncle. She waited until he had closed the door before she sprang to her feet. She looked in her full-length mirror and saw that the reflection looking back at her was that of a woman who had been crying all night. That was the last thing she wanted Brian to believe. If he thought that he was on his way over to her family's house to see her, broken down and miserable, while he told her that he was leaving her for another woman, he was sadly mistaken. She wouldn't give him the satisfaction. She couldn't. And what nerve he had to lie to her uncle and tell him that he had slept at his brother's house all night. He would never stay at John and Veronica's house since he wasn't that fond of Veronica. He would have been better off saying that he stayed at a hotel.

All night Kristy had stayed awake, going over her and Brian's life of the last few months. The signs were subtle but they had been there all along; the long hours at work, the sleepless nights, him always being on edge. But what really clenched it all together for her was the distance that had grown between them and throw in the fact that he'd recently stopped attending church. There was no denying that Brian was hiding something from her and until last night she hadn't been completely sure. That was until she confronted him with her worst fear and instead of denying it, instead of pulling her into his arms and reassuring her that she was still his one and only true love, he walked out of the house without even looking back.

With a new resolve, Kristy splashed cold water on her face and fixed her hair. She got some lip gloss and eyeliner out of her purse and put them on. Then as a finishing touch, she took a small bottle of her favorite perfume and sprayed some behind her ears, her neckline, and on both wrists. Now she was ready to face her husband and whatever it was he wanted to tell her.

Kristy walked into the living room and sat in the recliner, which faced the front door so she would be the first thing Brian saw when he walked in. He'd know the second he laid eyes on her that she wasn't some weak woman who needed a man to make her feel complete. She was already thinking of the things he would say and what her responses would be. "I hope he's prepared, because I sure am," she said to herself as she waited. One hour past by, but Brian hadn't shown up. An hour later, Kristy was asleep in the chair, still waiting.

Despite the fact that Lori had tried on six outfits and three pairs of shoes at the department store, she still got to Luigi's fifteen minutes early. The restaurant was crowded and the atmosphere was filled with conversation, background music and the most delightful aromas coming from the kitchen. And although Lori was hungry, her stomach had an awful case of butterflies. She wasn't sure if it was part of the pregnancy or plain old nerves. She began to take deep breaths to try and relax herself. She exhaled a little too loudly, and the couple at the next table looked in her direction. Lori smiled sheepishly and turned her head. That's when she saw him. Jimmy had just walked through the door. Lori checked her watch. Eight o'clock sharp. Boy, did he look good. He was wearing his dark blue jeans, white turtleneck, and red cable knit sweater. She loved the way he looked in red, and he knew it. He seemed to be pulling out all the stops, first the tulips and now the way he was dressed. Lori watched him as he spoke with the hostess. Then as if he sensed her presence, he turned and looked directly at Lori and walked toward the table. Lori watched him as he approached; he looked as nervous as she felt.

"Hi." The word sounded shaky.

"Hi," she answered back. Jimmy leaned over to kiss her cheek. He wasn't sure of how she would react, but to his surprise she didn't turn or back away.

Taking his seat across from her, he said, "I wasn't sure if you would be here. You never called me to confirm."

"And yet, here you are." She replied. The words were playful, not sarcastic.

"Well, I was believing or maybe hoping. I'm...I'm just..."—his eyes began to fill with tears—"I'm just so happy you came. I prayed, though. I asked God to move in your heart." He quickly wiped the tear away with the back of his hand and willed himself to relax before continuing. "So I take it that your being here means that you're willing to talk to me." A tear strolled down his face. Lori fought the urge to wipe it away. They still had a long way to go, and she was still unsure of how she was going to tell him her news. If she allowed herself to get caught up in the moment, she might blurt it out before she had a chance to hear what he had to say about their marriage.

"You said you wanted to talk, and so I'm here to listen. I'm not making any promises, Jimmy." She tried to sound firm, but her heart was already beginning to melt.

Jimmy had been thinking of how he would approach her, how he would start off the conversation. He hadn't expected to be this nervous. He reached for the glass of iced water, took a sip and then cleared his throat. "Well, I guess I should start by telling you I know everything." Lori jerked her head and looked directly into his eyes. How could he know? She hadn't told anyone but her father, and he wouldn't dare tell Jimmy. Would he? Unless he thought she wouldn't tell him. Panic filled her and she began to spill out the words.

"Jimmy, I was going to tell you. I was just waiting for the right moment. I actually thought tonight would be the perfect time. I hope—"

"It's okay. I understand," he interrupted. He reached for her hand.

"You do?"

"Yes, but I'm hoping I can change your mind, if it's not too late. I know a lot of time has passed, and we need to make a decision about this together." Lori was confused. What was he talking about? He couldn't be implying for her to have an abortion. Regardless of what their marriage was going through, Lori had decided an abortion was not an option. She simply didn't believe in it. She would be a single parent before she ever aborted a baby. She was suddenly becoming angry as it all began to make sense.

"Is this the reason you invited me to dinner?" she demanded. It was now Jimmy's turn to return her look of confusion.

"Lori, why are you yelling?" he whispered, looking from table to table to see if anyone was watching.

"I can't believe you would bring me to dinner to discuss something so personal. And here I thought you had really given your heart and life to God. How could you even contemplate something like this that is against the will of God? All day I thought you were serious about working on our marriage." Lori's eyes were brimming with angry hot tears. She couldn't believe she opened her heart to be hurt again by him. What a fool she was. A weak-minded fool.

"Lori, I have no idea what you're talking about. I am completely and totally committed to my life with God. If it wasn't for Jesus, I'd be dead right now. But He saved me, Lori, and I believe if we let Him, He can save our marriage as well. I know you were planning on leaving me, and I want you to know I'm not that same man anymore. I've really changed. Call it a divine intervention, but I've changed. And I wanted you to know that. I'm ready to do whatever it takes, even counseling. God's given me a new life and well, I want us to have a new life too." He fumbled in his pocket and pulled out a little black, velvet box.

"Lori, would you consider marrying me again—the new me—and giving us a fresh start?" Jimmy stood up and walked next to Lori and opened the box. Inside were two matching wedding bands. She looked at the bands and then up at Jimmy. She was suddenly feeling very overwhelmed with emotions. The room began to spin and her breath caught in her throat. The butterflies seemed to have increased in number and she felt very lightheaded. In the next moment, she collapsed right out of her seat. A gentleman from the next table rushed over to help Jimmy.

"Dampen your napkin in that glass of water," he ordered. Jimmy obliged and handed him the napkin. He placed the napkin across Lori's forehead with one hand and checked her pulse with the other.

Jimmy, observing his actions, asked, "Are you a doctor or something?"

"Yes,"—he smiled—"something like that." He began to lift Lori up as she came to. "She's okay, everyone," he announced and everyone began to return to their meals.

"Lori. Lori," the man called her name softly, as he gently tapped her cheek. Lori's eyes were wide open, but she wasn't focusing on anything.

How does this guy know my wife? Jimmy wondered. Finally Lori came back to reality and met his gaze.

"Dr. Anderson," Lori said quietly. He smiled at her. Both men helped Lori back onto her seat.

"I'm guessing you've had a little too much excitement. We talked about this in my office. You need to avoid any future occurrences like today." His tone was a professional one that held lots of authority. What did he mean avoiding too much excitement? And when exactly had Lori gone to see a doctor and for what reason? Jimmy's heart began to beat faster, and tiny beads of sweat lined his forehead.

"Would someone mind telling me what is going on? Lori, why have you been seeing a doctor? And why didn't you tell me that something is wrong? I am still your husband, after all." His voice raised two octaves. Dr. Anderson picked up on the hint that Jimmy was still unaware of his pending fatherhood status and excused himself back to his table. Lori wished he had stayed, just in case she lost her nerve or fainted again.

"Jimmy, I came here tonight wanting to tell you something, but not what you are thinking. That's why I got so reared up when you said you knew."

"Oh, dear Lord, no. Lori, are you sick? Please tell me the truth. We can beat whatever it is. I've been learning that Jesus bore our sickness and disease on the cross, so we can walk in divine health." She was so touched. He was genuinely concerned for her wellbeing. Instinctively she knew that somehow everything was going to be all right.

"Jimmy, I have been feeling sick for several weeks now. I finally went to see Dr. Anderson, and, well, there's really nothing we can do except—"

Jimmy broke her sentence with a deep sob. He grabbed her hand and squeezed tightly.

"It's okay." She was trying to reassure him so he'd calm down. By now, almost the entire restaurant was staring. She was sure that any minute they were going to be asked to leave. "I'll be back to my former self in about five and a half months." Another sob. He didn't yet understand. So she continued, "When the baby is born." Slowly the words took root, their meaning becoming clear. He looked at her with red eyes.

"What?" he asked.

"You're going to be a father. This isn't exactly how I intended to tell you tonight." She took a napkin and wiped his tears as her own now freely flowed from her eyes.

"Thank God. Lori, I thought you were dying. But you're just pregnant." He smiled and then said again slowly, "You're pregnant. And I'm going to be a dad." He began to cry all over again. And then he suddenly picked her up out of her seat and spun her around in a circle.

"Wow, dinner and a show. This was the best night. I love this restaurant!" a woman from a nearby table remarked to her friends, watching the scene with amusement.

———◆———

Kristy woke up to the ringing of the phone. Her left arm was stretched behind the back of the chair and her right hand was tucked in the seat cushion. She rose up out of the chair and headed for the kitchen. Her neck was stiff from sleeping in such an awkward position. *What time is it anyway*, she wondered.

"Hello?" she answered.

"Kristy. It's me, John. I've got something to tell you, but I want to make sure you are sitting down."

"What are you going to tell me, John? That Brian was too chicken to come over here and face me and tell me that he's leaving me for some other woman?"

"Kristy, stop it!" He hadn't meant to raise his voice. He understood her condition, but Brian was also his brother. Kristy was taken aback by his tone. He had never spoken to her like that. "Brian's been in an accident. It was a serious one. He's in surgery." Kristy was silent. All the anger, hurt, and fight were instantly gone. Accident? Surgery? How serious were his injuries? Her insides turned and a wave of fear overshadowed her. Not the same fear of losing Brian to another woman like she had had earlier. But losing him to death instead. She could defend herself against another woman but how does one fight death? Even if Brian decided to leave her, Kristy would recover, but what if he died? She wasn't sure if she could survive that. Brian was her world.

"Kristy, are you still there?" She couldn't speak. Courtney and Cynthia walked into the kitchen. Cynthia saw the blank look on Kristy's face and that her color was beginning to drain. Cynthia had had enough. Her niece should not have to be put through so much stress. It wasn't good for her or the baby. She took the phone from her hand as Courtney pulled a chair over to Kristy and forced her to sit down.

"Hello!" she said a little too loudly, anger in every syllable.

"Hi, Cynthia. It's John. Is Kristy okay? I just had to tell her that Brian has been in a serious car accident. I'm at the hospital now. Brian's in surgery, and they don't have any news yet, but they said it doesn't look good at all. I can come pick her up if she wants to come down here." The words pierced Cynthia's heart and she felt foolish for reacting so rashly.

"No, we'll bring her. Thanks, John. And don't worry. Now is the time for us to put our faith to action. Brian's going to be just fine." At the mention of Brian's name, Kristy looked at Cynthia and began to cry. Courtney reached out and hugged her. Cynthia placed the receiver on the handset. "Let's go." Within moments they were in the car. All the while Kristy sat in the backseat, she never stopped crying.

Taryn tapped her pen ferociously on the desk. She hated to wait. Nine o'clock meant nine o'clock on the dot, and not a minute later. Phil had been married to her sister long enough to know this about her. She checked her watch again; nine-fifteen. She would give him five more minutes, and then she was leaving, but not before calling him to tell him off. But just then the bell to the office rang. Taryn jumped up and walked to the door. She could see through the glass panel that it was Phil. She flung her arm up showing him her watch as she opened the door.

"I know, I know. But there was a really bad accident on my way over here. I was sitting in traffic on 287 for over forty minutes. By the time I got to the crash site, the tow trucks were getting ready to take the cars away. Or what was left of them anyway. The black Accord wasn't too bad but that little red Jaguar, if that person made it out alive, that would be a miracle."

The thought crossed Taryn's minds that Brian drove a red Jaguar but she dismissed it as quickly as it came. "Okay fine. Let's get to business." She turned her back and walked down the long corridor to John's office. The light was already on, and the files were piled on the desk. Phil, obviously impressed by the upscale décor of the office, let out a slow whistle. He ran his hand over the English leather recliner as he eyed the art deco paintings on the wall.

"Nice. Very nice."

"I'm glad you approve." The tone was very condescending. Phil caught the hint and retaliated.

"Exactly what bee has flown up your bonnet, Taryn? I mean, I didn't have to come out here tonight. I do have other cases I'm working on, but I put them on halt because you said this was urgent." When Phil scowled, the dimples in his cheeks were prominent.

"I'm sorry. I don't mean to sound so nasty. I'm just ticked that someone is up to something with Higher Thoughts. I really like these guys. They are down-to-earth, honest-to-goodness good guys. They don't deserve this." Hearing her explanation, Phil relaxed a bit. He understood. Taryn was nothing if not loyal.

"You sound as if you have proof already. What'd you find?" Taryn grabbed at one of the files and tossed it in front of Phil.

"I was here all day going through contracts and profiles, and I came across something interesting. D'Light is the company that decided not to renew their contract two months ago when it was time to re-sign. Now, just a few days ago, the owner of Creative View calls the office and says he is thinking of canceling his contract. He heard a rumor that Higher Thoughts was in trouble, and he didn't want the company his father worked so hard to build to go down with it. Under different circumstances, this wouldn't be so alarming except that Virgil has only been running the company since his father passed away a month ago. When he inherited the company, he had his lawyers add a clause to the contract that states if at anytime he loses confidence in Higher Thoughts' ability to successfully promote and maintain the companies positive image, they can renege on their contract without legal penalty or monetary damages."

"And your clients agreed to this?"

"They had no reason to be suspicious, considering they had been doing business with Virgil's father for the last eight years. They agreed based on the faith of the successful business relationship they'd established with Justin, Virgil's father."

"Poor, unsuspecting saps. See what happens when you are too trusting?"

"That's the problem with the world. There should be more people like the Felix family. What goes around, comes around, and they don't deserve it."

"Hey, do the two clients know each other?" Phil interrupted. His brain was already beginning to race. He could feel his heartbeat quicken, and there was a tingling sensation in his fingertips. He always got worked up over a good mystery.

Taryn, who knew this about him, excused his interruption and continued, "On the surface it doesn't appear that they do. But the point I was getting at is that they both bank at the same bank—Eagle USA." Phil's eyes dimmed.

"So what? A lot of people bank at that bank, including me. There's one every three blocks in New York City."

"Exactly. However, they bank at the same branch, and they have the same account manager." The light returned. Phil opened his briefcase and took out a yellow legal writing pad.

"Okay, I'm going to need all the facts so far. Let's start with the owner of Creative View." Taryn looked at his legal pad and shook her head from side to side incredulously.

"Really?" She asked pointing to the pad.

"What?"

"What decade are you living in? You don't have any kind of electronic recording device?"

"I like doing some things the old way. So sue me." He proceeded to write down the name of the companies and the names of the owners. Taryn rolled her eyes and began to go over everything she learned, from the beginning.

The rain was beating against the windowsill hard, but Lori barely seemed to mind. It was like a soothing melodic rhythm. She had been awakened by the smell of breakfast cooking downstairs and was in no hurry to get up. For the last three days, Jimmy had hovered over her, waiting on her hand and foot. She kept expecting to wake up from this dream. She was seeing a side of Jimmy that she had never seen, not even when they were first dating. His entire demeanor had changed. He was calmer, more helpful around the house, and he smiled more, a lot more. She had even caught him singing a few times. Whenever they talked about the baby, his whole face beamed. Lori herself, was even feeling better. The morning sickness wasn't nearly as severe as it had been just a few days earlier. She had started taking her prenatal pills, and the feeling of fatigue was even beginning to fade away. Although, this morning she didn't particularly feel like rushing downstairs. No, she was enjoying the comfort of her warm, cozy, thick duvet. Besides, it hadn't rained in over a month, and the sound of the rain really was mesmerizing. She rubbed her stomach and did something she had not done before; she began to talk to the baby.

"Hi. I'm…I'm your mommy." She heard her own voice crack and realized she was a little nervous. How silly was that? "I don't even know what to say to you, but over the next few months, you'll be getting bigger and I promise to do everything to make you feel comfortable. I'll eat all the right things, and I won't give in to any ridiculous cravings like rye toast with dill pickles like my mom did when I was inside her belly. Hey, you know that actually doesn't sound half bad. Oh, um, don't worry, I won't eat that. At least, not today." She giggled, feeling silly. *God, you are truly in the miracle business*, she thought.

"Good morning." Jimmy entered the room with a plate of breakfast on a tray. Lori eyed the French toast, bacon, and eggs, and her mouth began to water. She was suddenly feeling as if she hadn't eaten in a week.

"Oh, that smells and looks so good. But I need to brush my teeth first," she said, rising from the bed. Jimmy watched her walk to the bathroom. He couldn't believe how much love he felt for his wife and their unborn baby. He had been downstairs praising God for His love, mercy, and compassion. For helping his marriage to begin to reconcile, for changing Lori's heart, and for blessing them with this wonderful gift of life. Without realizing it, Jimmy began to sing "How Great Thou Art."

"What'd you say?" Lori yelled out, turning off the faucet.

Snapping back into reality, Jimmy answered, "I was just thinking about how good God is." Lori kissed him on the cheek and climbed back under the covers and reached for her food. Next to the glass of orange juice was her prenatal pill. How sweet.

"Lori, I was thinking, with the baby on the way, we are going to need more room."

"You're right. We can clean out the office and make that into the baby's room." She stuffed a forkful of the syrupy French toast in her mouth and savored the flavor.

"Or we can start looking for a house. Babies take up a lot of space, more space than what we have." Jimmy pulled out a paper from his back pocket and unfolded it. There was a picture of six houses on a cul de sac and children playing in the road. The caption on the top of the page read, "Westcliff Orchards, we not only produce beautiful homes, but ideal settings for families."

Lori read the words and looked up at Jimmy. He could read the question in her eyes and started to explain.

"Dean, from accounts payable at the job, told me about this new housing development he and his wife just moved into a few months ago. Oh, he said to tell you congratulations, by the way. Anyhow, he said they absolutely love it up there and the children really like the schools. All of the streets are named after a fruit. You get it, Westcliff Orchard?" When Lori didn't answer him, he quickly continued, "There are a few houses available and I'd like to take you by there. The schools are good, and the neighborhood is family oriented, better than around here, anyway." Lori was speechless. She hadn't put any thought into any of this yet. Jimmy continued to surprise her.

"Well, where is it?" was all she managed to say.

"About twenty-five minutes from here in Westchester County, a town called Harrison. We can go by today."

"But, Jimmy, it's raining outside."

"Lori, it won't be raining inside of the house. That's what's important." She thought for a moment, not able to come up with a reason not to go and then finally agreed.

"Okay. As soon as I'm finished eating, I'll get dressed, and we can leave."

"Great," he said and kissed her softly on the lips. This new home could be the icing on the cake and once again Jimmy felt an overwhelming sensation of gratefulness, mingled with a shimmer of fear, knowing that it was only by the grace of God any of this was happening. He'd come so close to losing everything. And as Lori enjoyed her breakfast in silence, Jimmy thought about how God used Dean to lead him to the Lord.

For weeks he had gone into the accounting office and begged the controller for advances on his paycheck. The gambling was becoming worse but the thrill and excitement he'd get from the risk was too much to pass up. And the drinking went right along with the gambling.

One day Dean had found Jimmy in the men's room vomiting in the stall. When Jimmy realized he was no longer alone, he tried his best to pull himself together. But it was apparent to Dean as soon as he saw Jimmy come out of the stall that he was hung over. Fear had gripped him and he begged Dean not to say anything to anyone. If he lost his job, Lori would leave him for sure. However Dean reassured him that he wouldn't say a word on one condition, that Jimmy agreed to have lunch with him every day for the next month. Feeling that he had no other recourse, Jimmy obliged. And over the month the two met in the employee lunchroom.

The first few days, Dean did the majority of the talking, mainly about his wife and their three children; Andrew, Alyisha and Alexander. It was his wife who thought it would be fun to give them all the same first initials. He also talked about his church and a lot of the services he attended. Usually that would have turned Jimmy off, but Dean spoke about his brothers and sisters in Christ with such excitement that it made Jimmy curious. And he also wondered why Dean had never asked about Jimmy's own spiritual status. By the third week, Jimmy had asked Dean if he could visit Dean's church. Of course Dean agreed and at that service Jimmy was greeted with such love by everyone.

It was unlike anything he had ever experienced in his life. The pastor had taught on the fact that every person who ever walked the Earth was created for God's pleasure, that each and every one of them, God had a plan for. And like the many members and parts on a human body, each person born has a special task, in this life. No one was born by accident or without purpose and that the only way to know who you are and where you fit into the master plan, was by having a personal relationship with the Master Himself. At the end of the service the pastor gave an alter call and Jimmy accepted Jesus as his Savior and Lord. God used Dean to point Jimmy towards gaining eternal life and now, quite possibly, He was using Dean again to point him to another new life, here with Lori and their unborn child.

It had been five days since the accident and the doctors had already performed surgery on Brian twice. He had a ruptured spleen, a broken leg, a broken arm, and there was evidence of head trauma. Although the operations appeared successful, and the swelling of his brain tissue had gone down, Brian was in a coma. There was no way of determining if there would be any permanent brain damage until he awakened, if he woke up at all. John had told Kristy everything the first night at the hospital as they waited for Brian to get out of surgery.

He explained that Brian was trying to replace lost business and that he was worried not only about the business going under but how he was going to be able to provide for her and the baby. Kristy was so ashamed and embarrassed by her behavior. She felt guilty that she allowed herself to believe that he was having an affair. And the last time they had seen one another, it had ended in that horrible argument. Knowing that encounter had led up to the accident was unbearable. Ever since John had called to let her know about the car crash, she hadn't stopped reliving that night. It very well could be the last time she'll see him like that again. Now that she thought about it, she realized she never gave him a real chance to explain. *And now if he dies, Oh dear God, please don't allow him to die*, she thought. There was no way she could live with herself. How would she be able to raise their child without his or her father? This was all her fault. If only she could go back in time. But what was the hope in thinking like that. She already knew that wasn't a possibility. Her only hope was to pray God's mercy for a miracle. Not for her sake, because she didn't believe she deserved God's grace. Not after the way she had behaved. But for their child's sake, and for Brian's. He was such a good man and, until recently, a wonderful husband. If only he had told her the truth. If only.

Phil had been trying for two days to make an appointment with Carol Landon, the woman in charge of Creative View and D'Light's accounts at the bank.

Unfortunately, she was not returning any of his calls. It could have had something to do with the fact that they had gone out once on a date, and he never called her for a second one. Phil had found her smart and beautiful but incredibly boring. This meant that he was going to have to try another resource, and he already knew where to start. Virgil Emerson was a member of Elite Physique, one of the most popular gyms in the area. It also happened to be where Al Rojas worked. And Al owed him big. Six months ago someone tried to steal Al's identity. Somehow they'd gotten a hold of Al's Social Security number, driver's license number, and bank account information. Their first mistake was that Al's legal name was Alyssa, and their second mistake was stepping into the bank and trying to make a withdrawal from her account for $2500. When the perpetrator showed up with the check, immediately the clerk alerted her supervisor. Since Alyssa made the regular deposits for the gym, everyone knew her at the branch. When the transaction took too long, the thief got antsy and left. The next day Alyssa contacted Phil. A week later the credit card company called her at the gym to confirm a purchase of a fifty-two-inch flat screen television. The credit card was issued by the same bank where she held her bank accounts. Phil managed to talk the bank representative into giving him the address of where the television was going to be delivered. That night Phil staked-out the address and had a friendly confrontation with Greg James when he showed up with some other purchased materials. The police took Greg away in a cop car thirty minutes later. And to thank the woman at the bank for cutting through the red tape for him, Phil took her out for dinner. Her name was Carol Landon. It was funny how life went around in a big circle. Phil dialed Al's number and told her exactly what he needed her to do. Of course, she willfully obliged. *What was that the church folks always said?* he asked himself. *God always provides a ram in the bush?* He smiled and tucked his phone away in his breast pocket.

Eric brought Kristy a cup of hot peppermint tea. She didn't look good at all, and he couldn't figure out why she was at work when the hotel was so slow. She should be home resting or at the hospital with Brian. Two months had passed, and he still wasn't out of the coma. All of his vital signs were strong, and the doctors couldn't figure out why he wouldn't wake up. But Kristy knew. This was her payback. Even though her aunt and uncle had told her time and time again that she wasn't being punished, she didn't believe them. She had allowed herself to lose faith in her marriage, and this was her reward. But Eric had made it his mission to snap her out of this depression. None of this was any good for her or the baby.

"So did I tell you that I finally asked Julia out on a date?"

"No, I don't think so." Kristy reached for the cup of tea and set it down on her desk. There was no sign of interest in her voice.

"We're going to the movies Saturday. We're going to see *Love and Taboo*. It's supposed to be a romantic comedy."

"I hope you have a good time." She never once looked up. She just continued to sip her tea. Eric's heart ached inside of him. He had known Kristy for a long time, and she was always very happy and upbeat. This whole ordeal was really taking a toll on her. He wasn't much of a praying man, but he had gotten to the point that he was making special requests on Brian and Kristy's behalf to the man upstairs. It couldn't hurt.

"Hey, how about you come along?" Kristy jerked her head up in a quick gesture with an expression of disbelief.

"Are you crazy? Julia's been after you for months, and at the first opportunity for her to be alone with you in a dark movie theater, no less, you're going to invite a third wheel?" Well at least he had managed to get a reaction out of her.

"You can be our chaperone," he teased. Kristy cracked a smile. The first one he'd seen in a long time. He continued, "Besides, it'll be good for you to get out and do something fun." Her smile faded and turned into a frown.

"How can I think about having fun when my husband is in a coma?"

"Kristy, it's not as if he's dead," Eric spluttered out without thinking. Stunned by his words, she dropped the tea and spilled it all over the desk. All of her papers were instantly soaked. Eric quickly rushed and grabbed some towels and began to absorb some of the liquid. "I'm so sorry," he apologized. Kristy began to cry.

Great going, Eric. Now you know why you're not seriously involved. You have all the sensitivity of a pencil, he thought to himself.

"Kristy, please forgive me. I didn't mean it the way it sounded." He tried again, reaching his hand out to console her.

"I know." She sobbed. "I just keep thinking what if he doesn't wake up. I can't imagine my life without Brian. He means the world to me."

"Kristy, how can you believe anything except that he's going to get better. You used to have more faith than anyone else I know. Do you really believe God would allow that to happen?"

"I don't know anymore, Eric. I allowed myself to not only doubt Brian but to doubt God as well."

"Is that possible? How do you lose faith in God? I mean, I'm not the most religious person, but I've never forgotten what I learned in Sunday School that God is a good God and that He loves me with all of my character flaws. And that each day He wakes me up is a new day to experience this beautiful world He created for me along with His love."

"Wow. I've never heard you talk like that before. You're like a closet believer or something," she joked mildly.

"No, it's not that." He paused a moment before continuing and Kristy waited patiently for him to get his thoughts together. "It's just that I know God has a major role to play in my life, but I'm just not ready to take Him up on it yet. But ever since the accident, I've been thinking about it more and more." He took his handkerchief and dabbed at her tears. She reached up and took the handkerchief for herself.

"Eric, don't you realize that if you wait until you're ready to give up this world, you'll never be ready? Once you make up your mind to give your life to the Lord and take a step of faith, you'll never want to go back to the ways of the world again." She chuckled as she heard the sound of her own words, trying to inspire someone about a relationship of faith with God. "I know I may sound contradictory now, but none of this has made me want to turn my back on God. I did this and this is the consequence of doing things my way."

"No, Kristy, you're wrong. All of this is God's mercy. If this... if this were really a consequence for your actions, well... Brian would have died the night of the accident." Eric had no idea where that had come from. He wasn't this insightful. Kristy allowed Eric's words to sink in. She realized that he was right. Everything he said was true. All of this time she had been feeling guilty and walking around depressed. But the fact was that God had spared her husband, and if He hadn't allowed Brian to die in the accident, He wasn't going to allow Brian to stay in the coma forever. She suddenly had an urge to be alone and fall on her knees and beg God to forgive her for everything. She had wasted so much time over the last few weeks crying and wishing she could go back and change the wrong she'd done. Now she needed to change her attitude and get ready for her husband when he woke up. She needed to go home and fix up their place and get things ready for the baby. She sprang to her feet and kissed Eric on the cheek.

"Thank you. I feel like you helped me to wake up out of a long sleep. And you're right. Brian's not dead.

I need to stop walking around acting as if he is. You know what, I'm going home. I think I need to spend some time alone with the Lord." She noticed Eric's look of concern and added, "I'm okay, Eric. Honestly. Suddenly I feel like me again."

"Does this mean you'll reconsider about the movies?"

"You're relentless." She grabbed her purse and walked out of the door. For the first time in months, she sensed something that had been missing in her life: hope.

"No, Brian's condition hasn't changed. The doctors are baffled, and I can't begin to tell you how discouraging that is. Of all people you'd like to hope that the doctors know what's happening." John pulled his tie off and threw it over the back of the chaise in their bedroom. Veronica immediately picked the tie up and hung it in his closet.

"He's going to be all right." She attempted to reassure him.

"I know. It's just a matter of when, that's all."

"Your mother called to say she plans on coming back this weekend."

"I wish she wouldn't." John slumped down on the chaise. His shoulders were very tense and suddenly he was aware of the fact that he was tired.

"John, how can you say that? That's her son in there. Besides, you've been at the hospital about four times this week yourself." Veronica began to massage John's shoulders. He was definitely tense. He loved the way she instinctively knew him. Immediately he relaxed a little bit, just from her touch.

"Again, you're right, but you still don't know my mother that well. No offense, but you're still relatively new to the family."

"Whatever," she snapped. Veronica hated when John tried to dismiss her input or feelings like they didn't matter. Seeing that he'd upset her, John tried to make amends and reach for her arm, but she jerked away. He didn't want to argue with her and leave things this way. If he had learned anything from Brian's accident it was that it's important to resolve every conflict immediately. Life was too precious for egos to get in the way. He jumped off the side and quickly blocked the bedroom entrance before she could walk out.

"I'm sorry."

"All I'm saying is that, as a mother, she has the right to be here."

"Of course she does." He attempted to reach for her hand again. This time she didn't resist, and he pulled her into his arms. She laid her head on his chest and John held her close. She smelled so good, just like gardenias. Having her in his life for the last two years had been wonderful. Even though he got the feeling that sometimes he felt more strongly for her than she did for him. He was sure that it was just his imagination playing tricks on him; at least, he prayed it was.

The house Jimmy had taken Lori to see was beautiful. It was the ideal two-story brick house with a white picket fence. It had a big front yard, and it was on a corner lot. The previous owners also had children, and there was a play-set in the backyard. The house was newly constructed, and the family had only lived there for eighteen months when the husband was offered a job in Europe with his company. They only had a month to pack and leave so they were looking for a quick sale. Lori had fallen in love with the kitchen, which was almost double the size of hers, with the island counter top in the middle, just like the modern homes she saw on television. The wallpaper was a yellow sunset with teak wood cabinets and recessed lighting. The living room faced the east and had plenty of windows. She liked that. But her only question was who was going to clean them all? Jimmy liked the wrap-around deck in the back. He could exit and enter onto the deck through the sliding glass doors from the dining room or from the living room. The den downstairs had an office already set up, which would be great for Lori to use when she got closer to her due date. The upstairs had two bedrooms and a full bath with a master suite. The master bedroom was closed off by double French doors that opened onto a small sitting area with a fireplace. She pictured herself sitting in a rocking chair putting the baby to sleep with a nice toasty fire crackling in the background. She couldn't help but to smile at the image. There were two huge walk-in, his-and-her closets, and past them was a master bath with a sunken tub, separate standing shower, two vanities, and a toilet. There was another door that opened into the bedroom with panoramic windows from the floor almost to the ceiling. To the left of the master was a second bedroom, which would be perfect for the baby, they both agreed. And further down the corridor was a third bedroom, which would serve as a guest room for family when they came to visit. Her mother was already planning to come and spend a week after the baby arrived. The house was perfect. Jimmy told Lori it had been God who set everything up for them, and she believed him. It was all just too coincidental. Since the house had been reduced for a quick sale, the realtor had strongly urged them not to take too long to think about it. Jimmy and Lori made an offer on the spot. They both borrowed from their savings and a small amount from their 401ks and put a sizable down payment on the house. They had closed within forty-five days. *So much has changed so fast*, she was thinking while she was sitting in the examining room for her check-up. She heard the door open and looked over her shoulder, expecting to see Dr. Anderson; it was Jimmy.

"Hey, what are you doing here?" She beamed up at him.

"The doctor's office left a message for you at home after you left this morning to remind you about the appointment. Why didn't you tell me?"

"Because it was in the middle of the day, and I thought you had to work."

"I'm on my lunch break. I would have been here earlier, but I ran into a little traffic. Did he already examine you?"

"Yeah, right. They give you a time and then show up twenty minutes after that."

"I heard that, Mrs. Adams." Dr. Anderson extended his hand to Jimmy. "We didn't get the chance to have a formal introduction the last time. I'm Dr. Anderson. And I'm guessing you're the husband."

"Yes, I'm Jimmy. Nice to meet you, Doc." Jimmy, realizing how cliché he sounded, quickly added, "I mean Dr. Anderson."

"It's okay. I've been called a lot worse." Turning his attention to Lori, he asked, "So how is our patient? Are you still experiencing morning sickness?" He took his stethoscope and began to listen to her heartbeat.

"No, I haven't. In fact, I've been feeling extraordinarily wonderful. Even the fatigue faded. It's like the complete opposite of a couple of months ago. I think now I have too much energy."

"Pregnancy is a funny thing, and no two are exactly alike."

"When is she going to start showing more?"

"Excuse me, what's your rush?" Lori shot Jimmy a look of unbelief. The fact was that Lori's abdomen had all of a sudden started to pop out. She was already wearing a few maternity outfits.

"I'm just excited to feel the baby move and kick, that's all. Lori's the only one who can feel the…what do you call them again? Flutters?"

"Will you settle for listening to the heartbeat for now?" Dr. Anderson offered. He couldn't help but to smile, he never tired of seeing the excitement of first time fathers.

"Really?" Jimmy's eyes were as wide as a child in a toy store. Lori couldn't help but laugh. Dr. Anderson put some warmed clear jelly on her abdomen and began moving the Doppler from side to side until he found it.

"Hear that? It's your baby's heartbeat." Dr. Anderson smiled. Jimmy looked at Lori and began to tear up.

"Oh, please don't start that again. Jimmy's more emotional than I am, Dr. Anderson."

"That's not uncommon. I remember when Agnes was carrying—"

"Dr. Anderson, I'm sorry to interrupt you, but we just got a call from the emergency room at Riverside Hospital. They have Kristy Felix there now. There's been an incident," a young woman called over the speakerphone.

"Excuse me for just a moment."

"Oh, I hope everything is okay," Lori called out.

"So do I." He closed the door behind him. Samantha was waiting for him in the hall. She was waving the phone in the air. "Okay, I'm here." He took the phone from her hand. "Dr. Anderson," he announced into the headset. The ER administrator began to give him a run down of information. Dr. Anderson kept nodding his head and answering yes into the phone. "I'll just finish up with my patient, and then I'll be right over." He hung up and exhaled slowly. He walked back into the examining room.

"Is everything okay?" Lori asked.

"I don't know yet, but it seems as if one of my patients has just been admitted into the emergency room. She's in her seventh month. She's had several strokes of bad luck lately. Her husband was in a car accident a couple of months ago, and he's been in a

Heaven Can Wait

coma. I'm afraid the stress of everything may have caused some complications."

"Oh, no!" Lori and Jimmy both said in unison.

"If you remember, just say a little prayer for them."

"Absolutely. If no one else believes that prayer works, I do." Jimmy looked at Lori and smiled.

Lori returned his smile and said softly, "Yes, it does."

"Mrs. Felix, do you know where you are?" Kristy tried to focus, but everything was blurry. Her head was pounding. She tried to remember what she was doing before waking up in this strange place. Slowly she remembered. She had been putting the wallpaper up in the baby's room. She wanted it to be all done so that when Brian got home, he would be so surprised. She was standing on the stepladder when the first pain hit. She had stopped for a few seconds, caught her breath, and continued. Then the second pain hit. It was much stronger than the first one and as she doubled over in pain, she lost her balance and was heading towards the floor. That was the last thing she could recall.

"You're in Riverside Hospital," a man's voice stated. She wondered how she had ended up in the hospital? Had she driven herself?

"How did I get here?" Her voice was barely more than a whisper.

"You must have called your aunt's number before you passed out."

"I don't remember doing that," she said with a note of panic in her voice.

"It's okay. Mrs. Felix, we've called Dr. Anderson and asked him to come right over. He's on his way, but right now I need to talk to you about the baby. We've had you hooked up to a fetal monitor for twenty minutes now, and we haven't been able to locate a heartbeat. We haven't performed a sonogram yet. We were waiting until you woke up."

"Wait a minute. Back up." She was fighting to sit up further on the bed. "What do you mean you can't locate the baby's heartbeat? What does that mean?" The monitor that was recording Kristy's heart began to beep rapidly.

"Mrs. Felix, please calm down."

"But you're telling me my baby…" She couldn't even finish the sentence. The words choked in her throat.

"Kristy," he said, using her first name for control, "what I'm saying is that we need to get you calmed down and get you prepped for a sonogram."

"I can't let anything happen to this baby, Doctor."

"We're going to do everything we can." But Kristy could hear it in his voice. It lacked hope.

The elevator doors opened, and John politely smiled at the couple and stepped inside. The woman sniffled, and as she reached for a tissue from out of her purse, she dropped the bag to the floor. Instinctively John knelt down to pick it up for her. As he handed her the bag, he looked at her closely for the first time. She had been crying, a lot. He couldn't believe that he had been so distracted and hadn't noticed when he stepped on

Heaven Can Wait

the elevator. Obviously they were just as distracted as he was.

"Cynthia, I didn't even notice you two when I got in." He handed the bag to Cynthia and extended his hand toward Courtney. He could see the glum looks on their faces. He knew nothing had changed with Brian because he had just left him. "I can't help but notice that something's wrong." Cynthia began to cry silently.

"It's Kristy," Courtney spoke slowly. "She's in the maternity ward."

John, suddenly alarmed, demanded, "What's happened?"

"She fell off of a ladder at her house a little while ago. The doctor's just told us…" Courtney's bottom lip began to quiver and he had to pause a moment before speaking the next words. "…ehat the baby's gone." His eyes welled up with tears.

"No. It can't be. Why is this happening?" The doors of the elevator opened, but for a second, none of them moved. John turned to them and asked, "Where is she now?"

"She's on the eighth floor. They want to keep her here overnight. They are going to give her something tomorrow to induce labor to…" Courtney raised his fist to his mouth, and the tears flowed down his cheek. John's head was spinning. First the company, then Brian, and now this. It was all too much. "Should I go upstairs and see her?"

"She's sleeping right now. As you can imagine, she didn't take the news too well." Cynthia managed to get a few words out.

"No, I imagine she didn't." He stepped off the elevator.

———◆———

Dr. Anderson dialed Lori's cell phone after he returned to the office. He had been in the profession for a very long time, but he never got used to situations like he had to just deal with. He wasn't looking forward to tomorrow and having to induce Kristy's labor to remove the baby. It broke his heart each time he had to perform the procedure, which thankfully wasn't too often. No matter, one time was one time too many.

"Hello."

"Lori, it's Dr. Anderson. I apologize I had to cut our visit short. I'd like for you to call tomorrow and reschedule with Berta, okay?"

"Okay. By the way, did everything work out with your other patient?"

"I'm afraid not. She lost the baby." Lori gasped in response to his news.

"Oh, that's terrible. First her husband's accident and now she's lost the baby."

"I don't want to bring you down. I shouldn't have disclosed that to you, but you're practically family. I just wanted to make sure you reschedule and to let you know today's visit will be no charge. Good-night, Lori." Lori managed to say good night back and closed her phone. She felt horrible for this woman. She thought back to only a few months ago when she found out about her own pregnancy. Thoughts of the moments came flooding back, and she felt a tinge of guilt. She remembered that for a brief moment, a very brief moment, she had thought about an abortion and leaving Jimmy and him not being the wiser about any of it. Now God had quickened her marriage, and she was overjoyed about becoming a mom. And here, this other woman's child and quite possibly her husband have been taken away without there being anything that she could do about it. Lori found herself on her knees praying earnestly for this woman she didn't even know.

Alyssa Rojas had been waiting patiently for her mark to arrive at the club. When he entered through the revolving doors and approached the desk, she smiled as the six feet-two inch man flashed his club pass at her. She could tell that he had recently been tanning. His skin was glowing. "How long have you been coming here now, Mr. Emerson? You can put your pass away." Up until this point, she had never done anything to catch his attention, but now she was on a mission. He winked at her and slipped it in his duffel bag. The gym had gone through a renovation, and this was the first day it had been open in two months.

"By the way, the whirlpool is being repainted. It's the only thing that isn't complete yet." She knew that he usually finished his workout by soaking in the whirlpool for a half an hour.

"Thanks, doll." She pretended to be flattered. But really, she hated being called pet names, especially "doll," it's not like they were living in the fifties. In her opinion, it was degrading to all females. He walked away with an extra strut in his step. She checked her watch: seven-thirty. He would be coming out at about nine-fifteen. She had to make it a point to be there when he walked out. She dialed Phil's number in the meantime and let him know the mark had just arrived. Phil was parked in the parking lot and told Al he was on his way inside. A few moments later, Al handed him a courtesy pass, which allowed him access to the whole facility. She watched him walk through the doors and toward the men's locker room. She could still see his Kelly green jogging suit through the window. This was all so cloak-and-dagger to her. She loved it.

Phil located locker number 347. In his bones he knew he was going to uncover something tonight. Things had gone cold for a while when Virgil Emerson decided to leave the country for a couple of months. He remembered back to the call he placed to Taryn when he had to tell her their investigation had to go on a temporary hiatus. She wasn't too happy. Oddly enough, Virgil's absence served a purpose. The whole time he was away, there hadn't been any more alarms at Higher Thoughts, that was until he returned three days ago. One more company called and requested to speak to Brian in person about the future of their account.

He was thrilled when just the day before Al called to let him know that Virgil had come by the club and being that Virgil was a creature of habit, he'd most likely be back the following day. Sure enough she was correct. Now hopefully he'd finally find something to help Taryn's clients.

He removed his little tool kit and popped the lock. The locker smelled of expensive cologne. He looked over his shoulder and seeing that he was alone, removed the designer gym bag. He unzipped the top and reached for Virgil's wallet. Nothing but hundred and fifty dollar bills in the fold. There was only one credit card. But it was the only one he needed: a black Centurion American Express card. Just flashing this told everyone in eyesight you had big money. Phil knew that people who carried this card traveled frequently, entertained regularly, and paid a $1000 annual members fee. No other business cards or important items could be found. Phil returned the wallet to its original place. He opened another compartment: a shaving kit with shower gel and deodorant. He turned the bag around and found a side pocket. He opened it up. He found Virgil's iPhone. He pressed a button. To his surprise the keypad wasn't locked. He scrolled through the names in the address book. He typed in L and went through the list of names. Carol Landon's name was there. He typed in P. George Parker, Olivia Parson, Greg Patella, and there it was, the connection he was looking for: Wendy Pawlak. He viewed the recent calls and saw that the two had talked just a couple of hours ago for over forty-five minutes. He was just about to put the phone away when his hand slipped, and he almost dropped it. Just by his touch, the keypad had scrolled down to another set of earlier calls, and he saw another familiar name. Could it be a mistake? If this person was who he was almost positive it was, things were about to get a lot more complicated. He had to talk to Taryn, but not over the phone. If he was right, something this big had to be revealed in person.

Kristy was tossing and turning in her hospital bed. She was dreaming that the baby was crying, so she walked down the long hallway toward the cry. The further she walked, the longer the hall became, until finally the baby stopped crying, and she found herself standing in front of a small closed coffin. When she awoke, she found that her pillow was wet. She had been crying in her sleep. Now fully awake, she heard a baby's cry in the distance and realized that was the cry she kept hearing in her dream. It was coming from the next room. She felt so numb. She needed Brian. She needed him to reassure her that everything was going to be okay. He'd always been able to cheer her up and give her a sense of hope with his words; that was up until the months leading up to the accident. Even so, she still knew instinctively that he'd have just the right thing to say to her right now. But there was only one problem with that: Brian couldn't speak to her. He couldn't even hold her close to him. And then she had a thought. She slowly removed her IV and unhooked herself from the monitors. She slipped into a pair of hospital slippers that were next to her bed and scooted out of her room. Being that it was so late, there wasn't anyone around. The night nurse had probably gone on break, or maybe she was helping one of the new mothers. Either way it didn't matter to Kristy. She walked to the elevator, and when it arrived, she stepped inside and pressed the fourth floor. She walked into Brian's room. He looked like he was just sleeping peacefully. Kristy ran over to Brian and threw herself onto his chest. She cried uncontrollably for about five minutes before she calmed down.

"Brian, I need you to wake up. Everything is a mess. I can't handle this all alone. The doctor's are going to take our baby away tomorrow." She sobbed deeply again for a few more minutes and then continued, "I'm so sorry. I know it's all my fault. Please forgive me. Oh, Brian." She looked up at his face to see if there was any hint of emotion. Nothing. She was sure she couldn't take anymore of this. For weeks there hadn't been any signs of change and none of the doctors who had talked to her had been able to offer a medical explanation as to why Brian was still in a coma . What if he never came out of the coma, what then? And if Brian wasn't going to wake up, what was the point in going on? Ever since the doctor told her about the baby's being dead, a thought had been growing in the secret place of her soul. The realm of her where there was no hope, only despair and condemnation mingled with guilt. Her flesh and her spirit had been at war ever since the thought was conceived and she was quite sure the fight was what had triggered her dream. The thought of suicide had seemed so unimaginable when it first introduced itself. But now, as she looked at her emotionless husband in light of the fears of tomorrow's procedure she'd have to face alone—the thought of never holding their baby, never celebrating all of the "firsts" with their little blessing and her husband—it all seemed too much to bear. And suddenly, the thought of leaving this world and all of the heartache it offered behind, no longer seemed wrong. It had all been a long strenuous last few months and she was tired, so very tired of it all. "Well world, if you wanted to find my breaking point, you've succeeded." She knew what she would do. She inhaled slowly and leaned over. She took Brian's face in her hands and kissed him on his lips. He was so warm to the touch. A tear from her eye fell onto his cheek. "No matter what happens, Brian, I love you." She returned to her room and spent the next few hours thinking about how she would spend her last day on earth tomorrow. After she left the hospital, she would go home, take a hot shower, put on some fresh pajamas, take a handful of sleeping pills, and drift off forever.

Morning came all too soon in the Wade household. Not that it mattered anyway; neither Courtney nor Cynthia had gotten any sleep. Cynthia spent most of the night thinking about Kristy's life. So much had been taken from her. Cynthia pleaded for God's mercy on behalf of her niece. If Brian would just wake up, he and Kristy could get through this together.

A few years ago one of Cynthia's closest friends Jennie had gotten pregnant. She and her husband, Reuben, were so happy. Jennie had just completed her first trimester and had gone for her monthly check-up. And just like Kristy, the doctor couldn't find a heartbeat. They hooked her up to a sonogram, and the baby's vital signs were flat-lined. Cynthia remembered Jennie telling her that she just looked at the baby on the fetal monitor, lying perfectly still. She was heartbroken even more so when the doctor's couldn't give her a good reason as to why the baby had died. One of the nurses had made an attempt to try to empathize with what Jennie must have been feeling by telling her that God doesn't make sense. The nurse told her friend Jennie she could never understand why God would allow some women to have a child when He knew they didn't want to be mothers. Since God is supposed to know all things, He already knew that these women would either give them up for adoption or even worse, neglect them or abuse them. Meanwhile, there are numerous women who desperately long to have a baby and be mothers and they either can't get pregnant to begin with or have miscarriages. Cynthia had never forgotten what Jennie said she told the nurse. She told her she didn't know why God allowed those women to become mothers, but she knew that one day they would have to stand before Him and give an account as to what kind of parent they were to their children. She went on to tell her that she did not know why God had allowed her to be without her child, but she did know that God had a purpose for her life. She chose to think about the goodness of God and how He spared her child from the pain of the world. Her child would never be hurt or in danger. Her baby was safe in heaven where he or she would only experience the love of God and the beauty of His creation. Jennie told the nurse that her baby would be without tears and know only laughter and joy. As much as she and her husband would have loved that child, they would never be able to promise a day without hurt, harm, or danger.

Jennie asked the nurse if she knew what God thought about her. Jennie said the nurse answered no. So she told her, "'I know the thoughts that I think towards you,' saith the Lord, 'thoughts of peace and not of evil, to give you a future and a hope.'" That's God's plan for His children. Cynthia wiped the tears from her eyes as she remembered this account and it brought her a sense of peace. She reached for her Bible and turned to read the familiar scripture from Jeremiah 29:11. Only the Word of God could bring comfort on a day like this.

"Are you absolutely sure, Phil?"

"Taryn, I'm a professional. This isn't idle gossip. Of course I'm sure." Phil rolled his eyes and clenched his fists. He purposely eyed the pots and pans hanging from Taryn's kitchen ceiling. He didn't like being second-guessed.

"I'm sorry. I didn't mean it the way it sounded. I just can't believe Veronica's name is in Virgil's phone. I could understand it if she had an active roll in the company, but she doesn't. She works as a real estate agent. I don't see a connection between the two. So what would Virgil be doing with John's wife's number? It can't be just a coincidence, can it?"

"Okay, so how do you want me to play this? Do you want me to follow up on the connection between Wendy and Virgil, or do you want me to find out what the connection is between John's wife and Virgil?"

"No, you keep trying to uncover what's happening with Wendy and Virgil. Leave Veronica to me." Taryn had a look in her eyes that was all too familiar to Phil. It was the same look his wife Anna got when she had an instinct that something was out of whack. Yes, the two were definitely sisters. Phil grabbed his coat and walked out of the kitchen. It was time to put the case into second gear. He just loved a good mystery. Taryn reached in her pocket for her cell phone. She looked up John's home number and pressed send. She hoped that John wouldn't be the one who answered. And as luck would have it, Veronica answered on the first ring.

"Hi, Veronica, it's Taryn Albright." She tried her best to feign enthusiasm in her voice as she spoke the words.

"John's not home," Veronica responded much too quickly. Veronica didn't like Taryn. She was smart, successful, beautiful, and, worst of all, single. She remembered the big production John made over getting Taryn's birthday gift last year. When she asked John why was he making such a big effort, he dismissed her like he always did. She had even gone so far as to ask him if before they met, had he and Taryn ever dated, which he had emphatically told her no. Although she believed him, she couldn't help feeling like there was some connection. And she didn't like it, not one little bit.

"Oh, that's okay." Taryn tried to make her voice sound lighthearted. "I just wanted to tell him that we may have found a connection between the owners of D'Light and Creative View. Phil's setting up a meeting with a reliable source today to confirm everything. I'm sure John's filled you in on what's happening." Veronica began to cough abruptly.

"Excuse me," she said as she gasped for air.

"Are you okay?" Taryn asked with mocked concern. But she knew she had just gotten her confirmation. Actions speak louder than words.

"I'll give John your message. I need to take care of something. Bye, Taryn."

I bet you do, Taryn thought to herself, smiling as she flipped her cell phone closed and ended the call.

Kristy had managed to fall asleep but was woken up when the nurse came in to take her temperature and blood pressure. She noticed Kristy had removed her IV and made a disapproving noise with her teeth, as she simultaneously shook her head in disapproval. Dr. Anderson walked in, and she let him know what Kristy had done and announced that she was going to get a clean needle to hook her back up.

"Hi, Kristy," he spoke. Kristy didn't bother to look up and face him. He understood but continued anyway. "In a few minutes, the nurse is going to come back in and hook you up to the IV. Then she's going to add Pitocin to your patch. Pitocin is a synthetic form of a hormone called oxytocin, which comes from the pituitary gland. It will stimulate your uterus, causing contractions." Kristy wasn't listening. She was deep in thought, remembering the first time she had met Brian.

It was an unseasonably cold and windy May day. She'd gone into the city to meet her aunt at Higher Thoughts office on Lexington Ave between 46th and 47th streets.

Just as Kristy had reached the building's door, a strong gust of wind blew and forced the door to swing back so quickly that she lost her footing and stumbled. Her hands immediately launched forward, and there was Brian, catching her before she could fall. She looked up in relief, and the first thing she noticed was his beautiful smile and straight, white teeth.

"Whoa, are you okay?" he asked, reaching to pick her purse up.

"I'm…I'm good." She stood up and straightened her skirt and jacket. She caught a reflection of herself in the glass door and could see her hair had come partly undone from its bun. She quickly tugged the pins out and let it fall down to her shoulders.

"Better," Brian commented, and Kristy blushed.

"Well, thanks for keeping me from falling," she managed to say.

"Oh, I'd gladly do it again." He flashed his smile once more. Kristy's stomach did a flip.

"Do you have business here?" he inquired. Kristy looked at him with a sideways glance and he quickly added, "What I mean is, I can help you find your way if you need me to. I work here and know everyone in the building."

At this, Kristy smiled relaxing her guard a bit. "Actually I'm meeting my aunt who has an appointment with the president, Richard Felix. I'm sure you know him, right?" she asked mockingly.

"I most certainly do. He signs my paycheck."

He held the door open to allow Kristy to walk before him. Once inside, he showed her to the elevators and took her to the top floor labeled Executive Level. The doors slid open, and they both stepped off of the elevator. He stepped quickly in front of her to open the glass door for her. She walked through another doorway as he held it open for her a second time. He tapped the desk to get the young man's attention who was sitting at the reception desk reading a designer magazine.

"Hi, Bri, I was just checking out the new AD we did for—"

"It's okay. Is Mr. Felix in with anyone?" Brian had interrupted to ask.

"Yes,"—he looked down on his log and then back up at Brian and Kristy— "a Mrs. Wade."

"Your aunt?" Brian guessed with a cocked eyebrow. Kristy nodded yes, and Brian motioned for Kristy to follow him down the hall. She wasn't sure who he was, but two things were clear: one, he must of held an important position there since the receptionist let him go back without questioning him, and two, he was definitely trying to impress her. Brian knocked on the door twice, not waiting for a response before opening it.

"I have Mrs. Wade's niece here," he announced when he saw the agitated look on Richard Felix's face. Kristy walked in and shook his hand and then kissed her aunt on the cheek. "Kristy, it's been a long time since I've seen you. You've turned into a stunning young lady. Must run in the family." He smiled at her, and Kristy noticed that there was something familiar about his smile, something that reminded her of the man who had come to her rescue just moments earlier. "Thank you, Mr. Felix. It's good to see you again."

"And I see you've met my son, Brian."

"Well, not formally. We haven't exchanged names as of yet." Brian gave her a mischievous smile. And once again her stomach did a somersault. And at that moment, Kristy instinctively knew, their chance meeting wasn't chance at all but destiny being fulfilled.

Just then Kristy felt a sharp pain that brought her back to the present. The nurse had just stuck the needle in her hand and was about to start taping the tube on her arm.

"Kristy, do you have any questions about what I've just told you?" Kristy closed her eyes and shook her head no. She just wished that it was already over.

"I'll be back to check on you in about an hour or so." He backed out of the room and closed the door behind him. For the moment she was once again left in the room alone. She knew what she had resolved to do the night before but there was no peace about her decision. And she was afraid that if she did go through with the act, her family, and maybe even God, would never forgive her. During one of her Bible studies a while back she remembered reading the passage that God doesn't put more on us than what we can bear. God wasn't out to destroy her. What if all of this, everything that has happened, had been for another reason? What if God wanted to do something in their lives that could only come from what looked like a mess? Wasn't He God, Sovereign and Almighty, and able to make all things good? For the first time since everything had happened, Kristy realized that she had been looking at her surroundings through natural eyes. She had allowed herself to wallow in doubt and self-pity instead of exercising her faith. The Bible admonishes that we are not to lean to our own understanding but in all of our ways we are to look to God and He will establish our path. But somewhere along the way she had forgotten this. Shame and embarrassment were filling her heart but she wouldn't turn away from God, not anymore.

"Lord, I know I haven't been too pleasing in your sight lately. But I just want to tell you...I want to tell you I'm sorry. I'm sorry for everything. I know I should have been a better wife. I should have prayed for Brian instead of condemning him for not going to church and not talking to me. I should not have allowed my feelings and thoughts to create all those scenarios in my head. I let you down. I let Brian down. I let my baby down before I ever got a chance to be his or her mother. Please forgive me. I'm ready to come home now, where I can never disappoint anyone again. But if there's any hope, if there's a possibility that maybe I can have another chance to make things right, I promise to not mess up again. I'm asking for your mercy Lord, please... please tell me what to do." She said the prayer aloud, and she meant every word. She instinctively placed her hands on her stomach and sighed heavily. Just then, a woman with short, curly gray hair walked in on a cell phone, without even bothering to look up.

"Heaven can wait. No, no," she said more emphatically, "I said Heaven can wait." She looked up and met Kristy's gaze who was staring back with a startled expression on her face. "Oh, excuse me," she said and turned around and walked back out just as quickly as she had entered. Before the door could even close all the way, Courtney and Cynthia walked in.

"Did you hear what that lady just said?" Kristy asked them, still puzzled by the encounter.

"What woman?" they asked at the same time.

"The woman on her cell phone who just walked out as you were walking in."

"Kristy, there wasn't anyone walking out when we got here."

"What are you talking about? You literally just passed each other. The door didn't even close when she left, right before you walked in. You must have seen her," she insisted.

"Sweetheart," her uncle said gently, "we didn't see anyone." Courtney wasn't sure if Kristy was making any sense. Kristy got off of the bed and wheeled the IV with her as she rushed past her aunt and uncle to look out in the corridor for the woman. She looked to the left and then to the right. Not seeing anyone, she walked to the corner to the elevators, but she only saw a few nurses standing there.

"Excuse me, did you see a woman in a white suit with short, gray hair on a cell phone just now?" The nurses all began to shake their heads no and went back to what they were doing. Kristy walked back to her room. She knew that her emotions had been completely out of whack lately, but she was sure that she hadn't imagined the unexpected visitor just a few seconds ago.

"Are you okay?" Cynthia asked with a look of concern when Kristy reentered the room.

"I know I might not sound as if I'm making sense, but I know what I saw." She looked from her aunt to her uncle and saw the obvious incredulous looks on their faces.

Courtney cleared his throat before he said, "Sweetheart, you're not even allowed to have your cell phone turned on in the hospital."

He eyed Cynthia and she chimed in, "How 'bout we get you back into bed." She noticed her niece's appearance. She was definitely fatigued; her eyes looked somewhat glazed over, and her hair was a mess. Kristy didn't want to fight with them so she climbed back onto the bed. But she knew what she saw, and more importantly, she knew what she'd heard. "Heaven can wait". It wasn't just a coincidence. The weight and the reality of the words hit her, as if God Himself had spoken them into her soul. She'd just finished praying and asking God if there was any distinct possibility for her to have a second chance at life with Brian, any chance at all when the woman entered. And then a sudden thought came to her. She knew it didn't make any sense in the natural, but she had a strong sense, an unction, that God was about to do something, something amazing.

"Uncle Courtney, would you mind doing me a favor?" Her voice had a trace of excitement as she asked the question.

"Of course." He was ready to oblige any request she had right now. Anything to make this as easy on her as possible, as if there could be anything capable of doing that.

"Please go and get the nurse. I want them to—no—I *need* them to check for the baby's heartbeat." A look of fear crossed his face; he tried to recover, but Kristy had seen it. She reached for his hand and held it in hers for a moment and looked at him with loving eyes. "I'm not in denial, Uncle Courtney. Please," she begged. He looked at his wife, and with a tearful nod of her head, she encouraged him to do so. He placed Kristy's hands on the bed and rubbed her shoulders and turned toward the door. A few moments later, the nurse came in the room and immediately began to fire off a list of opposing statements. But finally, with great reluctance, she gave in when Kristy told her she had every right to make this request and that she'd speak to the head nurse if necessary.

Nurse Prakash, as her name badge read, went to go get the equipment, but not before placing a call into Dr. Anderson. If the results were the same, which she knew they would be, she didn't want to be responsible for making the ultimate decision. Dr. Anderson asked her to wait until he came back from visiting one of the other newly delivered mothers, which Nurse Prakash was only too glad to agree to. Moments later he was outside of her room. He drew in a deep breath before pushing the door open.

"Kristy, I've been told you'd like to be hooked up to the monitor again. May I ask why?" His words were gentle, not judgmental in the least.

"Dr. Anderson, I know how this may sound, but I know everything is going to be all right. I prayed, and I believe...no, I *know* God is going to answer my prayer." Out of the corner of her eye, Kristy could see her aunt wiping tears from her face.

Dr. Anderson cleared his throat, "Kristy, I don't want to discourage you from having faith, but you do realize that when you were hooked up, we monitored you for several minutes without any signs of the baby's heartbeat?" He leaned in a little closer. "I know this is hard for you, especially with your husband in the condition that he's in right now, but I'm really not in favor of doing this. It's only going to cause you additional heartache."

"Dr. Anderson, are you telling me that you will not do this?" Kristy met his gaze; he could see the determination in her stare.

"No, that's not what I'm saying." He straightened up and took a small step back from the bed.

"Then I'm ready when you are."

He asked the nurse to bring over the electronic fetal monitor and then proceeded to attach the band around Kristy's abdomen and then attached the transducers. He turned the machine on and waited. The log showed that Kristy was having contractions, very mild contractions, but no heartbeat registered. Kristy had seemed so sure, and he was disappointed to be proven right. He watched the monitor for a few more moments before speaking again.

"I'm sorry, Kristy. The result is the same as it has been since yesterday when you were admitted. Now try to get some rest. You're already having mild contractions. In a few hours, if they haven't increased, we will give you another dose. One way or another, we're going to deliver the baby tonight." He turned on his heel and walked out of the room.

The silence was thick and very uncomfortable. Cynthia took a seat next to Kristy and smoothed her hair. "It's going to be okay. I know it doesn't seem like it now, but it's going to be okay."

Kristy's response surprised her aunt and her uncle: "Yes, Auntie. Yes it is." Kristy was smiling.

The colors here were unlike anything he had ever seen. They were so rich and vibrant, almost as if he were seeing them for the first time. And there was a sense of peace that he'd never experienced before. He felt loved, protected, and joy—such great, great joy. It was all around him, penetrating his soul from the inside out. Was everyone here aware of the same thing? Did they share his feelings too? He looked around and noticed there were no shadows anywhere. There was light, a glorious brilliant light all around him, not one shadow. It was the strangest thing. He wanted to stay here forever and keep talking to the man dressed in the white suit. When he spoke it was like music, every note in perfect harmony. No, he never wanted to leave this place; he liked it here. He was safe and there was no more fear or doubt or questions about tomorrow. Except one: what about Kristy? Who would look after her and help her with the baby? He loved her so much, but somehow that seemed dim in comparison to the love he felt in this place. No, he'd stay right here, maybe even forever.

———◆◆◆———

Taryn's phone call had caused Veronica to go into a full-blown panic. If the connection between the two companies had been discovered, it was only a matter of time before she was found out as well. Veronica had never meant for any of this to happen.

It had all begun when she'd run into Todd Pace at the Marriott in downtown Houston, Texas. Todd was attending the same black-tie gala at the Museum of Fine Arts for a fundraising event that she and Brian were also attending. It was some weird twist of fate. Todd and Veronica, had been married, though briefly. The marriage was over almost before it began. Todd was manipulative, domineering, and condescending. But when he wanted, he could also be extremely charming, making her feel like the most beautiful woman in the world. After six months of the roller coaster marriage, crying to her mom and sister every other day, they finally convinced her to leave him. Of course, Todd hadn't taken the news too well. He threatened to come after her and bring her back to him no matter what. Veronica believed it wasn't just a threat. No, Todd meant every single word. It was for that reason that when the divorce was finalized, she moved from her home in Aurora, Colorado, to a small town in Westchester, New York, cut her shoulder-length hair to a cute little bob, went from a natural red head to a brunette, and changed her name from Emily Schneck to Veronica Van Raalte.

Back in Colorado, Emily had been a fashion designer, so when she moved to New York, she enrolled in classes at the Fashion Institute in the city. In her third semester, she met John on the Metro North one day when her heel got caught in the space between the train and the platform. John had noticed her when she got on the train at the Hartsdale station. He was looking down when the doors opened, and the passengers stepped inside. It was her three-inch red heels that first caught his attention. Who wore three-inch heels on the train? But when he looked up and got a full view of her, it all made sense. She was beautiful—one of the most beautiful women he had seen in a long time. She could be a model, even though he didn't think she was more than five-six, five-seven at the most. John thought about approaching her but decided not to. There was a sadness in her eyes that sent a message that she was only interested in making new friends, and so instead he just admired her from afar as she took a seat a couple of rows behind him. But when her heel got caught just as they were getting off at Grand Central, John didn't hesitate to assist. And that was the way it all began.. John fell in love immediately, and they were quite happy up until that trip to Houston.

It hadn't mattered what Emily had done to alter her appearance; Todd knew instantly who she was when he saw her checking into the hotel. The funny thing was that he had turned down his boss's invitation to go to the event initially, but she hadn't taken no for an answer. Todd was to be her escort, and since Angela Conti wasn't used to being denied anything, he obliged reluctantly. He was happy that he did.

    Emily was alone at the registration desk, and he wasted no time getting behind her at the counter. When she turned away to head for the elevators she practically knocked him over. She began to issue a flood of apologies and stopped in mid-sentence. During the quick exchange she hadn't looked at him; she only reached his shoulders. But her stomach suddenly felt sick as she smelled that all-too familiar cologne, and subconsciously she knew. She looked around to see if there was anyway to get around him. There was no where to make a quick escape. Defeated, she looked up and confirmed what she already knew. It was indeed her ex-husband. Todd was only too happy to see the sheer look of terror on her face when their eyes met one another. He grabbed her elbow, leading her to a remote area in the lobby. She tried to break free but he was so much stronger than her. He tightened his grip and she had to walk quickly to keep up with him. Her heart raced and she could feel her breathing pattern accelerating. This was her worst nightmare coming true. Once they'd reached the other side he pulled her close to him and kissed her roughly on the lips. She was in the midst of raising her hand to slap him when he caught it in mid-air and advised her not to even think about it. He demanded to know where she'd been for the last few years and when it seemed as though she wouldn't talk, he threatened to find the tall dark handsome man he'd seen her all cozy with and tell him about their past.

She looked him square in the eye and filled him in on everything. How fortuitous that she was married to a man whose company was one of his direct competitors. He wasn't sure exactly how this piece of information was going to benefit him just yet but he knew he would think of something. Now that he'd found her, he wasn't about to lose sight of her again. So he arranged for her to keep seeing him, privately. She agreed to do whatever he asked out of fear since she had never told John anything about her true past, including the fact that she had been married once before. As far as he knew she was from New York and her parents, like his sister-in-law, Kristy's, were deceased. A few months after their reunion, Todd began forcing Veronica to help him get information on accounts from Higher Thoughts. She enlisted Rose, John's assistant and started sharing information with Todd. When he found out their largest account was Creative View, he began a plan to wine and dine the owner Justin Hargraves. However, Justin would have no part in it. He was happy with Higher Thoughts and was loyal since he had been high school buddies with the founder, Richard Felix. So Todd turned his attention to other accounts. D'Light was next on his list, and that had been far easier to steal away. Angela was incredibly pleased with Todd's new clients, and the bonuses were nice—oh so nice. Then six months ago, Todd was informed that Justin Hargraves had passed away, and his son Virgil was taking over the company. Virgil was young, immature, and greedy for money. Todd had Veronica arrange a meeting between him and Virgil. Over dinner at Le

Cirque, a very upscale French restaurant in New York City, Todd offered Virgil a two hundred and fifty thousand dollar bonus to sign with Blazon Marketing. He also convinced him to put a clause into their contract, the very clause that was going to allow him to eventually leave Higher Thoughts. But Todd didn't want Virgil to leave just yet. He wanted to steal a few more accounts and then go in for the kill. He figured what better way to get back at Veronica than by putting her husband's company completely out of business. Then he'd tell John Felix exactly who he'd married—Todd's leftover—a traitor named Emily Schneck from Aurora, Colorado.

For some reason Lori had woken up that morning with the woman in her mind. She didn't know her name; only the fact that this woman's life was in turmoil. Her husband was in a coma, and now she'd lost her baby. Lori caressed her stomach and again felt a moment of regret at how she initially responded to the pregnancy.

She looked at the clock and found that she had less than two hours to get into the office. She trudged out of bed, slipped into her comfy house shoes, hurried to the bathroom, took a quick shower, and dressed all in less than twenty minutes. Lori then headed downstairs into the kitchen. On the counter with a folded note with her name on the outside was a tall glass of orange juice and her prenatal pill with her vitamins. She already knew what the paper said; he'd been leaving her the same love note every morning: "I love you. Have a blessed day in

Christ, and keep our lil' one safe." She smiled and read the note like she did every morning to the baby. She was getting into the habit of talking to him or her on a regular basis. She knew some people found it silly, but Lori was convinced that her unborn child could hear everything that was happening in the outside world.

As she thought about this, she suddenly had another thought. It was far out there, but the more she thought about it, the more she was sure that the idea wasn't her own but an inspired thought from God. She walked around the island counter and reached for the cordless phone on the wall. Her assistant answered on the first ring, and Lori informed her she was going to be a little late. She grabbed her car keys and headed to Riverside Hospital. If babies could hear what was going on in the outside world, maybe people who were in comas could, too.

Lori racked her brain to remember back to the day when she was in the examining room at Dr. Anderson's office. What had the nurse said the woman's name was? Felix. Yes, her last name was Felix; she was certain of that. Now what was her first name? Kerry? Kristen? No, that was close, but it didn't ring true. Lord, if this is you, please bring her name back to my memory. She prayed but there was no answer, no sounding of trumpets or flashes of lightening spelling out the name in the sky above, like she had seen in so many movies. Still she couldn't shake the feeling like this was what she was being prompted to do. Maybe if she took her mind off of it, it would come back to her. Aware of how quiet it was in the car she turned on the radio to her favorite station. An advertisement for an upcoming concert in the park had just finished and the disc jockey was back on the air.

"Hey New York, we have a special caller on the line who wants to give her mom a birthday shout out. Go ahead sweetheart." A little girl with the sweetest voice came on and said, "My mommy is the best in the whole wide world and I want to wish her a happy birthday from me and my daddy." Lori smiled at the small voice. She figured she was probably about eight years old or so.

"Tell everyone your mommy's name and your name so she'll know it's you." He chuckled.

"She'll know it's me just by my voice, but her name is Wendy." From the background you could hear another voice telling her to go ahead and give her name. The little girl huffed and spoke again, "And my name is Kristy." If Lori hadn't been driving and wide-awake, she would have thought she was dreaming it. The answer had come in such an unexpected way. If she had had any doubt moments ago, it was all gone now. God was definitely up to something.

It had only been two hours since Kristy had been given the injection, but the contractions were already getting stronger. She had hoped that the baby's heartbeat would have been picked up on the monitor, but when it hadn't, she didn't allow herself to get discouraged or allow defeat to creep in. To her it only meant that God wasn't ready for the miracle to be revealed yet, the miracle that she was now certain He was going to preform. When she finally acknowledged God and abandoned her own fears, it was as if her faith had been given a super charge. She knew her aunt and uncle as well as Dr. Anderson probably all thought she was in denial. But Kristy had a peace like she hadn't experienced in a very long time. The scripture came back to her, "God will perfect everything that concerns you." That pertained to her unborn child and her husband who was currently in a coma. What had Eric said to her that day at work? *God hadn't spared Brian from the accident just to allow him to stay that way forever.*

Kristy sucked in her breath as she felt another sharp pain. Her contractions were indeed intensifying. "Okay, Lord, it's all up to you now," she whispered in a voice only for her own ears even though she was in the room alone. Her aunt and uncle had left to get something to eat and would be returning shortly. She looked out her window and noticed that the earlier gray, cloudy sky was beginning to brighten up. To the east, the sun was shining through the clouds as they were slowly moving in the sky. Kristy chose to view the weather as a sign from God. He was working everything together for her good and His glory. She took comfort in this and laid her head on the pillow and closed her eyes. She was suddenly very tired and wanted to rest while she could.

"So do you think Kristy really saw someone?" Courtney asked his wife as he handed her the cup of coffee and buttered roll he had just purchased from the hospital cafeteria.

"I believe she thinks she saw someone. But I don't see how we wouldn't have noticed the woman, especially if she were dressed in a white suit and was on a cell phone. I don't know. Maybe the drug they gave her earlier caused her to drift off to sleep, and she dreamed it." Cynthia took a sip of the black coffee and twisted her face in disgust. It was bitter, just like everything that was happening to her only niece. Too much had been taken away from Kristy, and it just didn't make sense. Why was God allowing all of this to happen? She knew better than to think or question God like this, but sometimes she just didn't understand His ways. But then again, wasn't that what trust was all about? We walk by faith and not by sight. That's what 2nd Corinthians 5:7 said. This wasn't the time to question God. No, this was the time to stand in faith knowing that God loved Kristy and Brian more than anyone could imagine. He even loved their unborn child who had died before having a chance to live. Yes, every aspect of their lives was in His hands, and He's a big enough God to see them through everything, whatever that entailed.

"Courtney, would you mind going to see Brian with me? I realized I've been so focused on Kristy that we haven't even gone to see him since we've been here."

"Of course. Here, let me take that." He reached for the cup and tossed it into the garbage. "Tea?" he asked her.

Cynthia smiled in spite of her hurting heart. Courtney knew her so well. "Please," she answered. He quickly returned, and the two headed to the fourth floor to see Brian.

When they reached the room, they were surprised to find a woman kneeling at Brian's bedside. Courtney and Cynthia exchanged a puzzled look and watched the stranger who was clearly praying. The question formed on his mouth, "Who is she?" Cynthia shrugged her shoulders and took another step into the room. As her heel clicked on the tiled floor, Lori stopped praying and looked up to find that she was no longer the only visitor in the room.

"Hi." It was Cynthia who spoke first. "Do we know you?" Lori wasn't sure if the couple were his parents, although they didn't quite look old enough. She stood up with a little difficulty, and Cynthia noticed her round belly. Clearly the woman was pregnant.

"Hi, I…this might look…uh, strange." Lori stumbled over her words as Cynthia waited patiently for the young woman to collect her thoughts. Courtney stood guard behind his wife, silently observing the scene.

"Let me try this again. My name is Lori Adams. I was in Dr. Anderson's office yesterday with my husband," she quickly added, then continued, "when he got the call about this man's wife. Dr. Anderson and my father are very close friends, and he shared that his patient was in the emergency room and that her husband was in a coma. As Dr. Anderson was leaving the room, he told us to pray for them. It bothered me all night, and I've been praying for them since I've heard what happened. I can't explain it, but I felt led to come here today and just pray out loud with him."

Cynthia's expression softened as the young woman explained her presence in the hospital room. "I'm Cynthia Wade, and this is my husband, Courtney. Brian is married to our niece Kristy" Courtney reached out his hand and shook Lori's.

"Thank you, Lori, for being obedient, especially since it probably seemed like such a strange thing to do. But I've learned that everything God prompts us to do is for a reason."

Lori's eyes were glistening. "Over the last few months, I've come to know God more through my husband, Jimmy, and I realize how blessed I am and how merciful God is. He healed our marriage when I thought it was dead. I see my husband transforming before my eyes." Lori wasn't sure why, but she was sharing her life with these two complete strangers as easily as if she'd known them all of her life, but she went on, "I would have never believed it possible. Jimmy was drinking and gambling, lying to me all of the time, and now," she looked up at them as a single tear traveled down her cheek—"and now he's reading his Bible instead of drinking, praying instead of gambling, praising God instead of lying. I know if God could do that for Jimmy then He can do anything. That's what I told Brian before I began to pray, and I'm sure that wherever he is, he heard me."

Then Lori stood up and shook their hands again and excused herself. Courtney sensed God's presence in the room and knew beyond a shadow of a doubt that God was working.

———◆◆———

Brian looked around, taking in the view. He was in a field with the most gorgeous flowers he'd ever seen. There was a family of three under a tree, just a few feet away, having a picnic. Although he couldn't make out the faces of the husband and wife clearly, he could tell they were happy and, yes, peaceful. But the baby, the baby he saw as clear as day. The baby had a head full of hair, the same color as Kristy's. And the eyes were big and brown. The baby was kicking and waving its arms, almost as if he or she was praising God. Then he heard the baby laugh, and Brian's heart melted. He turned his attention to his friend in the white suit with the voice he could listen to forever. "Who are they?"

"Don't you know?" the man asked. Brian didn't take offense to this. He was getting used to the way his responses were sometimes evasive. Brian understood that his friend, the man in the white suit, wanted him to search inside of himself for the answer instead. Kind of like a teacher and their student. Brian started to shake his head no, but then it came to him. He was sure of it.

"That's me and my family, isn't it?" Without saying a word the man nodded his head, confirming Brian's assumption.

"But then what are we doing here, and how can I be here if I'm over there? I don't understand."

"Brian," The familiar angelic voice spoke, "you've been given a special and rare gift. Just over that mountain—" the man pointed somewhere off to the distance—"are the gates of Heaven. You're spirit is here, but you're body is back on Earth. And although we're not quite ready for you to come home, what happens now is your choice. Our Lord has allowed you to see a glimpse of the life still ahead for you. He's working a miracle right now, and even though He wouldn't get the glory if you were to come home now, the choice, like I said, is yours."

"But how did I get here to begin with?"

"Don't you remember? Look up."

Brian looked to the sky and noticed a flock of sea gulls, flying in perfect synchrony. Their wings open and closed at the same time and when one flew higher they all flew higher to the exact height. Then without warning, they all flew in different directions, the harmony broken. That was when he remembered. He was on his way to buy some of Kristy's favorite chocolates before stopping by her aunt and uncle's house to see her. That's when the car in front of him ran into the guardrail and had spun out of control. There was no time to react before he ran into him. He remembered calling out God's name before the collision and that was the last thing he remembered. As soon as the memory finished playing out in his head, the sea gulls came back together and continued to fly in synch as though they'd never stopped.

Brian looked at the family again, and his heart suddenly ached for Kristy. So many things he'd left unsaid.

He had allowed his pride to cloud his judgment. She deserved better; she deserved to know the truth. No, he didn't want to come home like this, not without completing all the things God had for him to do. Not before getting things right with Kristy. And he also agreed that God wouldn't get the glory if he died from a car accident. What had the man said? He was being given a special and rare gift, a second chance to make things right.

"How do I get back?" The man smiled at Brian's question.

"Just open your eyes."

Brian blinked a few times and tried to open his eyes. They felt as though they had tiny weights on them but he finally pried them opened. Everything was blurry. He could make out two figures standing next to him, but he wasn't sure who they were. One thing was for sure: he was no longer in that place, the place where he felt great peace. And his friend in the white suit was gone as well. He tried to speak but nothing came out, there was no sound. He swallowed a few times and tried again.

"Hello." His voice sounded weak, and his throat was so dry.

"Why are you telling me hello?" Cynthia asked looking at her husband. But Courtney was not looking at her. He had his hand covered over his mouth and was shaking his head from side to side. Although she couldn't see his mouth she was sure he was smiling because it reached all the way up to his eyes. Cynthia positioned herself to see what he saw and was completely caught off guard. Brian was awake and staring up at the two of them with such a look of bewilderment. Her heart beat faster and she was filled with excitement. She jumped to her feet and shouted a little to loudly, "Thank you, Lord." Her voice was elated. Courtney walked over to Brian's side and patted his shoulder, partly just to make sure he wasn't dreaming. He had a lump caught in his throat but managed to say,

"Welcome back, son."

Brian recognized their voices. Even though the light hurt his eyes, he tried to focus as he looked around the room. He was disappointed to find that his wife was not there. He wondered if she was still upset.

"Where's Kristy?" Cynthia's heart sank at the question and she opened her mouth to respond, but nothing came out. Courtney cleared his throat and began to relay to Brian the events that had taken place over the last thirty-six hours. He told him how as Kristy was finishing the final touches on the border in the baby's room, she felt a sharp pain and fell off the ladder she was using. The next part was harder for him to say, he took his time when letting him know that as a result of the fall, the baby had died. Cynthia was by his side the whole time Courtney spoke. She was mixed with emotions. Partly in shock that Brian was awake and without any apparent negative side effects, and partly grieved that he had to be confronted with such bad news so soon after his recovery.

"But that's not possible. I've seen…" Brian started but then stopped. They probably wouldn't believe him anyway. He needed to be with Kristy. She shouldn't have to face this without him. He'd already been so distant, and he wasn't going to make that mistake anymore. "Take me to her." He tried to sit up on his own and realized he needed some help. There didn't seem to be any strength in him at all. The room spun around a little bit and his head was beginning to hurt from the light. But it didn't matter; nothing was going to stop him from getting to Kristy. For all he cared, they could give him a wheelchair and he'd roll himself into her room.

"Cynthia, would you get the doctor, please?" Courtney asked.

"There's no time," Brian opposed. His voice was stronger now. There was no questioning the determination in his voice. With or without the doctor, he was going to his wife. Brian waved Courtney over with his hand. Against his better judgment, Courtney rushed to Brian's side and helped him to his feet. Cynthia handed him a robe and watched Brian as he slipped it on. In less than five minutes, he was standing in the doorframe of Kristy's room.

She was sound asleep and was as beautiful to him as ever. He felt as though he hadn't seen her in years instead of weeks. A smile formed on the side of her mouth, and he wondered for a brief moment if she was dreaming. Then without much of a notice, she opened her eyes and looked right at him.

"Hi," she said so casually that it was as if the last few months had never happened. She didn't seem surprised to seem him at all. Brian wondered if she'd had some premonition while she was still asleep. Perhaps his friend in the white suit had visited her as well.

"Hi, yourself." He took a step into the room. The lump in his throat was aching. She reached her hand out to him. Brian seemed to have found some hidden strength and broke free of Courtney's grip.

"How was your nap?" she teased. He couldn't help but laugh. She was truly amazing, and he was incredibly blessed. He wanted to climb on the bed right beside her and hold her tightly. Instead, he leaned over the bedrail and kissed her tenderly on the lips. She reached up and placed her hands on either side of his face and kissed him back. A long lingering kiss, full of excitement, joy and of course, gratefulness. Brian's standing in front of her was a clear sign that God was giving her a second chance. She felt stronger than she had in a long time.

"Kristy, it's all going to be okay," he whispered loud enough for only her to hear.

"I know." She smiled back at him. She really did, with every fiber of her being.

John hung up the phone and clapped his hands in victory. Brian was finally awake. He reached for the phone and called his mother to tell her the news, but just as he was about to dial the number, the door to his office opened unexpectedly. Veronica walked in, closing the door behind her. John could tell something was wrong. She looked terrible. He stood up and rushed to her side. She managed to say his name and then broke into tears. He held her close until she finally calmed down. "Baby, what's wrong?"

"I don't... I don't even know where to start. You're going to hate me, John." She searched for the words and mustered up the courage to continue: "I've done something so bad that I don't think you'll ever be able to forgive me." John could feel his heartbeat begin to race as he tried to imagine the worst. But he didn't press her; he remained calm and waited for her to continue. He'd learned from Brian and Kristy the dangers of reacting too quickly, and he didn't want to make the same mistake. Whatever it was, he was going to make every effort to remain calm and not loose his cool.

"John, maybe you should sit back down."

Dr. Anderson was happy to see Brian with Kristy when he entered the room several hours earlier. Kristy had been in hard labor for the last four hours, and it was time for her to start pushing. Brian was standing next to her, coaching her through each contraction. His strength looked like it had completely returned. He held her hand and counted down as the contraction leveled off.

"Kristy, the head has crowned. With the next one, I need you to give it all you've got." Dr. Anderson motioned for his nurse to bring Kristy some more ice chips.

Kristy sucked in her breath as she felt the next contraction coming. She squeezed Brian's hand and pushed hard for ten seconds. She breathed in and out and waited for the next one. *God, I know that you're with me. Thank you, thank you for watching over me right now,* she prayed silently. The next contraction hit, and she pushed as hard as she could.

"You're doing great, Kristy. The head is out." Dr. Anderson could see a head full of auburn hair. Brian kissed Kristy's hair, which was damp with perspiration. She reached up behind her and rubbed his back just as another contraction came on. Again she pushed, and the baby's shoulders were out.

"Just a little more," Dr. Anderson told her. With the next contraction, she mustered up every bit of strength she had and pushed with all of her might. The baby was out. A beautiful, very tiny, baby girl, perfect in every way except one: she wasn't breathing. Kristy was sure that any moment the delivery room was going to fill with the sound of her daughter's cry, announcing her entrance into the world. But the only cries she heard were that of her and Brian.

She had been so sure God was going to prove everyone wrong. Even now when her baby girl was so still and quiet, with no trace of life in her at all, Kristy remained calm. Their daughter was beautiful and her life was a gift from God, all life is. Kristy's eyes never looked away as the nurse cradled the baby in her arms. "I want to hold her." Kristy stretched her arms out. The nurse cut the cord and handed the baby to Kristy. She was even more beautiful up close, ten tiny fingers and toes that were not quite as long as Kristy's index finger. Brian bent down beside his wife and daughter.

"Lord, I don't understand," he sobbed, "but I'll praise you. No matter what, I'll praise you for this little one and my wife and for giving us this moment to be together."

Kristy nuzzled her face in the baby's neck. "I love you so much," she whispered. "I'll love you always and forever." Kristy felt the moisture of her tears run onto the baby's neck. Then she felt a hand brush against her face, followed by a small gurgle sound in her ears. Kristy pulled away and saw the baby was looking right at her. She snapped her head and looked up at Brian. Their daughter was alive. God had answered their prayers. Both Brian and the baby had made a miraculous recovery in the same day.

"Hello little one-" The words caught in her throat. Kristy was crying now, but the tears were of joy. "I'm your mommy." Brian looked at their daughter closely. She was smaller and had a lot less hair than what he remembered from his dream, vision or apparition. He wasn't sure what it was exactly but he remembered every detail. He'd remember that for as long as he lived, he was sure of it.

"Well, I'll be." Dr. Anderson stood in amazement. The nurse reached for the baby, and Kristy reluctantly handed her over.

"We'll bring her back soon, Mrs. Felix. We need to clean her up and weigh her." The nurse reported. She kept looking at the baby as she walked. The nurse couldn't explain what she'd just witnessed. What was supposed to be a stillborn baby was very much alive.

Dr. Anderson, still in shock, gathered his thoughts and spoke. "And I need to do a check up and check her lungs. She's about a month early, and the lungs are the last thing to fully develop. I'm probably going to want her to stay in an incubator for the meantime until I have some answers. We'll have the staff pediatrician check her out as well." He spoke each sentence slowly. Never in his thirty-three years had he ever encountered a case like this. There was no faulty equipment or misdiagnosis. At least three different machines had been used to search for the baby's heartbeat. All three couldn't have been wrong. And although he'd prayed for a miracle, he hadn't really believed it would happen. His medical training and science didn't allow him to fully believe in miracles, until now. There was no denying what had taken place in that delivery room. It was a phenomenon that he was willing to acknowledge that God somehow intervened. He looked at Kristy and Brian who were now hugging each other in a close embrace. He remembered Kristy's expression several hours earlier when she asked to have one more monitor reading. She looked so sure of the results and even when nothing had changed, she didn't look disheartened. Had she known then, and if so, how? His own eyes glistened with tears and he excused himself from the room but not before congratulating the new parents.

"Dr. Anderson, thank you." Brian extended his hand to shake the doctor's. Dr. Anderson shook Brian's and sort of chuckled and said, "I can honestly tell you that

I'm not the one who did anything. I'm still trying to figure out what happened." Kristy, still holding on to Brian looked up at him and said, "I know exactly what happened; we'd call it a miracle, but to God it was simply an answer to a prayer."

Kristy was taken back to her room while Brian, who had changed out of his gurney and into scrubs, went to share the news with Courtney, Cynthia, and John, who had arrived shortly before Kristy had gone into the delivery room.

John had been sitting in the waiting room, just thinking. Right as he arrived, they were taking Kristy into delivery. There hadn't been enough time to tell Brian all that had transpired, and even if there had been, he wasn't sure he wanted to go into it at that time. John had hugged Brian for a long time and cried tears of joy before Brian left the room with Kristy. He had been so happy to have his brother back, that was all that mattered at the moment.

But as he sat there and waited for everything to be over, he took in the weight of all that Veronica had told him. He knew all along that something had changed in their marriage after their trip to Texas. He wished she had told him the truth from the beginning. All this time she had another life he knew nothing about. He felt like such a fool. He'd asked her if she even loved him, and she swore she did. But how could he be sure? He now knew that the only reason she had confessed was because Taryn's brother-in-law had found the connection between the companies and Veronica's number in Virgil's phone. Had that not been the case, he wondered if she would have ever come clean. He didn't know what was next, but he'd asked Veronica to give him some time to think. It was all too much to process at once, and now that he knew what was happening, he needed to come up with a game plan to save Higher Thoughts.

Unfortunately, even though the way they had lost the accounts was underhanded, nothing illegal had been done. Therefore, he couldn't press charges against Blazon Marketing. But that didn't mean he wasn't going to fight to save the company his father had started thirty years ago. And once Brian had taken some time to recuperate and grieve over the loss of the baby, the two of them would figure out exactly what to do. Until then, if need be, he'd sell everything he owned to carry them over while looking for accounts to replace the lost ones.

Over the years, he'd met so many people and done so much networking that he was sure they'd be able to get back on their feet again. He had to have faith. Not that he ever gave God priority in his life, but God had certainly gained his attention. He had already brought Brian back to them; he would somehow bring Higher Thoughts out of the red.

John looked up as the swinging doors to the waiting room bumped open. Brian, dressed in his blue scrubs, was walking toward them. John had to be strong and be supportive of his brother. Brian had taken on so much of the responsibility over the last several months, which was how he'd ended up in the hospital. Now it was time for him to be the big brother and take the reigns. They would recover from this, and Brian and Kristy could try again.

But as Brian got closer, he didn't look like a man who'd helped his wife to deliver their stillborn child. He was probably in shock. Brian was now standing in front of them. Courtney and Cynthia were on their feet, ready to console him. Brian looked from one to another and could no longer contain himself. He cried with a sob that came from deep down inside. John was first to grab his brother.

"It's okay, Brian. We're here for you."

Brian broke away from his embrace, shaking his head. "It's a girl. Praise God, it's a girl!" he shouted, not caring if the whole hospital heard him.

"Oh my Lord." Cynthia clasped her hands over her mouth. Could it be? Could this really be true? First God had brought Brian back just in time for Kristy to deliver their baby, and now He'd given them another miracle in the life of the baby. Cynthia felt her knees going weak and began to rock, but Courtney was right there to catch her.

Above and beyond what we could ever ask or think, that's how God wants to answer our prayers, he thought to himself.

Brian let them all take it in and then let them know that they could see Kristy shortly. The baby was being tested, but she'd be in the nursery soon, and they'd all be able to see her, too.

"This might be too soon, but have you named her yet?" John asked.

"As a matter of fact, we did. Her name is Genesis. Genesis Phylicia Felix."

"Genesis, the beginning." Courtney said in awe.

"Yes. God in his mercy has given us a new beginning."

Now almost a year later, Brian looked at Kristy, who seemed to be somewhere deep in thought. She had tears in her eyes, and he intuitively knew she was saying a prayer. Knowing exactly how she felt, Brian took her hand and kissed it. The sensation of his touch brought her back to reality and she smiled. A soft wind blew, and she looked down into the stroller. Genesis was all snuggled up inside, sleeping soundly.

Any minute now, they were going to light the tree. It was hard to believe Christmas was in just three weeks. But Kristy had been given the best gifts, in the lives of Brian and their daughter, who each day was more amazing than the last. Even though she was only a little over four pounds when she was born, she had grown in size and weight over the last year. Another miracle was that she hadn't experienced any deformities or slow developments from being born early. Yes, they had a lot to be thankful for.

So much had happened since her birth and his recovery in the hospital that day. When Genesis turned four months old, they decided to have her christened. Courtney and Cynthia along with John and their mother attended the church service that morning. Genesis was dressed in her white gown and bonnet and looked so angelic as Pastor McKnight sprinkled her head and prayed over her. She didn't even make a sound. There was another couple that was also having their baby christened. Theirs was a little boy, and he looked younger than Genesis.

After the ceremony, the congregation congratulated the families, and for the first time Cynthia noticed the other woman. She looked very familiar. She went through her mental memory file to try and place where she'd seen the woman before. And then it came back to her. It was Lori, the woman from the hospital room. She was no longer pregnant, and her short, dark, curly hair had grown out. She imagined the handsome man next to her was her husband, Jimmy. Cynthia approached the family and could see that Lori was a petite little thing without her belly. Jimmy was tall and dark haired. He had kind eyes and a warm smile. Lori was pleased to see Cynthia. She recognized her immediately. "Hi," Cynthia greeted them with excitement.

"Hi, Cynthia. This is my husband, Jimmy." Moving the blanket away from the baby's face, she said, "And this is Caleb."

The baby boy was dressed in a little white suit and had the curliest black hair she'd ever seen on a baby. He looked up at her and smiled as if he knew something they all didn't. Cynthia had to love the irony—Genesis and Caleb, the beginning and faithful.

"I'd like to introduce you to my niece." Before Lori even had the chance to respond, Cynthia took her hand and led her, with Jimmy following close behind, over to where Kristy was speaking to another couple.

"Excuse me," Cynthia interrupted. Kristy turned away from the others and faced her aunt. She was greeted with awestruck smiles. Lori hadn't known that the woman standing next to her was Cynthia's niece. For the first time, Lori took a good look at the man to the side of Kristy, and saw that it was him, from the hospital room, only he looked much better now. "Kristy, Brian, I'd like you to meet Lori and her husband, Jimmy. Their son was just christened, too." They exchanged congratulations, and something in Lori's voice was familiar to Brian. His arms broke out with goosebumps even though the church was quite warm.

"Have we met before?" He had a puzzled expression on his face that made Cynthia and Lori both laugh.

"Brian, this is the young woman I told you who came to the hospital to pray for you. Lori, moments after you left, Brian woke up, just in time to be with Kristy as she delivered their baby."

"Thank you, thank you." Brian patted her shoulders. Kristy embraced her in a hug, and tears stung her eyes.

Lori let the magnitude of the moment sink in. She couldn't be sure if her obedience to go to the hospital that day led to Brian waking up out of his coma, but somehow she sensed she played a role in it all. One thing she was learning was that everything God directed His children to do was always for a purpose, even if it didn't make sense at the moment. Lori found it funny that they'd been attending the same church for months now and had never crossed paths until that day. As they continued to talk and compare post-pregnancy stories of sleepless nights and ungodly feeding times in the wee hours of the morning, Kristy sensed a connection with the couple. Something told her they were going to be friends for a long time to come.

"I just went back to work a couple of weeks ago, and it's been hard. Each morning I have to say goodbye, it breaks my heart, and I count the hours until I'm back home with her again. The only thing that gives me some comfort is knowing that she's with my aunt and uncle, who've taken turns with her until we find a nanny." Kristy confided in her new friend.

"I still have a couple of weeks before I go back. And luckily for me, my boss is allowing me for the first year to work part time in the office and part time at home. So I'll get to spend more time with the baby." Lori reported back.

"Wow, that's great." Kristy was slightly envious.

Seeing the look on Kristy's face, Lori had to laugh as she added, "I'm sure it has to do with the fact that my boss is happy to be a new grandfather."

"Oh, you work for your dad." The understanding came and Kristy now laughed too.

"Yes, the hard-nosed boss, Howard Kline, has turned into a huge teddy bear since his grandson's birth."

"Howard Klein? The same Howard Klein who's the CEO of Chips with Bytes?" Brian had been having his own side conversation with Jimmy, but the mention of Lori's father's name caught his attention.

"Yes, do you know him?" Brian shook his head with a smile that got bigger and bigger.

"My brother, John, has a meeting with him tomorrow. We own an advertising company, and we've been after your father's account for a long time. Just last week, he agreed to meet with John and a couple of his board members." If Higher Thoughts got the account, it would be the biggest account they've ever had. It would more than make up for the accounts they'd lost, and since they were still in the process of finding new clients, they could give Chips with Bytes a lot of extra attention.

"Well, I guess I'll see him there. I'm the Director of Sales and Marketing, so I told my father I would attend the meeting. I think I can put in a good word for you." She smiled back.

Brian turned to his other side and gave in to the uncontrollable urge to hug his brother standing next to him. John didn't seem to mind the embrace and patted his brother's back heartedly in response. Kristy watched the exchange and reached passed the two for Veronica's hand, giving it a gentle squeeze.

Veronica felt blessed to be here, sharing this moment with them. She never dared imagine another holiday season with the Felix family, not after what she'd done. But it was a time of miracles, thankful hearts, and forgiveness. She and John had made a lot of progress and continued their weekly sessions with the Christian counselor at church.

When John first learned of what Veronica had done, it very nearly crushed him. He'd been too stunned to do anything but ask her to leave his office. Only days later, the feelings of hurt and betrayal weren't as prominent as they had been when she first confessed. After all, she could have left without confronting him about her role in the whole thing. On some minute level, John knew she had done what she did to keep him, to save her marriage.

In the end John had chosen to forgive her. It wasn't an easy decision though. He had searched his heart long and hard. And although he didn't feel that she deserved his forgiveness, the question that he couldn't get away from was, had Jesus left out any sin when he died for the whole world? Could there be any act of disobedience not forgiven? Of course the answer was no, but he knew he couldn't forgive her of his own recourse. So he'd prayed and by faith, he released it all over to his Savior, casting every hurt and pain on him. John still remembered the wave of peace he felt wash over him and fill his body as he let it all go. Similar to how he now felt watching Brian who had moved back near Kristy and was hugging her around her waist. The look of nostalgia as Brian stared into Kristy's eyes was almost tangible. John could only imagine what Brian was thinking at this moment.

Yes, God had done a work in their lives, Brian thought as he stood there at Rockefeller Center in the cold December air, beholding the people he loved most in the world. *And when He gets involved in the affairs of His children, he really gets involved.* The verse that he and Kristy had over Genesis' crib, Jeremiah 29:11, came back to him as he thought about it all: "'For I know the plans I have for you,' declares the Lord, 'plans to prosper you and not to harm you, plans to give you hope and a future.'" And the future was exactly that: full of hope.